DISAST

The middle third of the twentieth century was just ending when worldwide disaster struck! Two heavenly bodies were detected approaching the Solar System that contained Earth and her siblings. Named after the astronomer who first sighted them, these were called Bronson Alpha and Bronson Beta. Bronson Alpha, the larger of the two rogue planets, was going to strike the Earth! Over the next four years, several nations constructed arks that would safely carry passengers to Bronson Beta, upon which ancient cities had been seen, indicating that it was habitable.

On the second pass of the two planets, Earth was destroyed, reduced to rubble by Bronson Alpha. As the remnant of the larger planet continued on its course through the galaxy, the arks traversed space to their new home. The Americans, led by Cole Hendron, sent two arks to Bronson Beta. Soon, they learned they were not alone: A group of Russians, Japanese and socialist Germans had also successfully reached Bronson Beta – and they were hostile.

Both camps moved into the ancient cities of the original inhabitants of Bronson Beta. These were domed, built to endure the long cataclysm that had propelled their world into deep space. The cities were filled with superhuman technology. But they were empty.

The Asiatics attacked the American group by cutting off their power, leaving them to freeze in the long, cold, dark winter of Bronson Beta, which had settled into a stable if eccentric orbit around the Sun. When the leader of the Asiatic camp was assassinated, the coalition fell apart, and was defeated by the Americans and British, who had been prisoners of the Asiatics.

Other Westerntainment Books

The Marvel Timeline Project, Part 1 by Jeff Deischer and Murray Ward
The Way They Were by Jeff Deischer
The Adventures of the Man of Bronze: a Definitive Chronology (3rd ed.) by Jeff Deischer

THE GOLDEN AGE series by Jeff Deischer
The Golden Age, Volume II: Mystico
The Golden Age, Volume III: Dark of the Moon
The Golden Age, Volume IV
The Golden Age, Volume X: Future Tense
The Golden Age, Volume XI: Bad Moon Rising

ARGENT series by Jeff Deischer
Argent
Night of the Owl
The Superlatives
Strange Days
Modern Times
Mystery Men

THE STEEL RING series by R. A. Jones
The Steel Ring
The Twilight War

THE BROTHERHOOD OF SABOURS series by Wes T. Salem
The Brotherhood of Terror Book One: The Shadow of the Sund
The Brotherhood of Terror Book Two: The Reavers of Kargh
The Brotherhood of Terror Book Three: The Red Brotherhood
The Heart of the Universe

AGENT KEATS series by John Francis
Skull & Bones
Chinese Puzzle
High Hopes

BEYOND

WORLDS

COLLIDE

Jeff Deischer

a **WESTERNTAINMENT** publication

BEYOND WORLDS COLLIDE
published by Westerntainment
Denver, Colorado, USA
Westerntainment.blogspot.com
westerntainment@gmail.com

Beyond Worlds Collide copyright 2016 Jeff Deischer

Based on *When Worlds Collide* and *After Worlds Collide* by Philip Wylie and Edwin Balmer, which are in the public domain

ACKNOWLEDGEMENTS

Thanks to:

Jerry Putsche, who suggested a "Star Trek" approach to the Micorites;

The Fulton Street Irregulars for their valuable feedback: David Webb; Peter Garcia;

Art Sippo, for his support and friendship;

And, as always, my parents for their support.

This book is dedicated to
all the authors who are the
inspirations for my writing,
both large and small.

This work was inspired by
When Worlds Collide
and
After Worlds Collide
by Philip Wylie and Edwin Balmer

BRONSON BETA
known area

o = Olympus-Gorfulu
x = American landing site
scale = [2000 mi]

BEYOND

WORLDS

COLLIDE

PROLOGUE

When Stars Collide

More than a million years ago, the people of Micor lived in an enlightened age. Reason, not faith, was the principle that guided them. Disease was all but unknown, and food was plentiful. Crime was rare, war rarer still. Society functioned like a clock, each piece playing its part.

Occasionally a part went bad, and had to be replaced. Improvements to the fabric of society were not always successful. And, of course, some parts worked harder than others, while still others received more attention because they were the visible pieces. No society is perfect, and that of the planet Micor had its flaws, despite its spiritually elevated state.

For a thousand years, society functioned in this manner, until, one day, Micorian astronomers detected a rogue star. They calculated that the object would pass near enough their solar system that it would tear away most of the outer of the eleven planets there. Some might even be destroyed. Only time would tell.

The same astronomers who had sighted the rogue star, which had been named Borak by the Micorites, estimated that two hundred years would pass before the arrival of the nomadic object and catastrophe struck Micor.

The people of Micor had two hundred years to save their civilization.

A genius by the name of Lagon Itol devised a plan whereby his race might be saved. He realized that the entirety of the population of Micor could not be saved from destruction. There were simply too many people. Thus, the first part of his plan was to reduce the population of the planet. Over those two hundred years, ticking away like seconds on the timer of a bomb, this dwindled from one billion to two hundred million.

The second part of Lagon Itol's plan was to construct domed cities that would survive the proximity of Borak and any perturbation of orbit that might follow. Micor's astronomers had calculated that their planet stood a fair chance of surviving the passage of Borak. Its orbit would certainly be disturbed, but perhaps it would resume one stable enough to maintain life. Micor's fate was uncertain, and would not be known until Borak grew near. The inhabitants of Micor prepared for the worst.

The domed cities were grouped as five, one each at the cardinal points of the compass, geography permitting, with one in the center that served as the headquarters of the group, providing heat and light to its subordinate quartet.

As Borak approached, the Micorites huddled in their domed cities. But as the rogue star grew nearer, it became clear that the worst scenario Lagon Itol had envisioned would come true. Micor would not be spared.

The people were unlucky. In half a year, their planet would be on the other side of the solar system and they would have survived the catastrophe. But such was not to be.

And so, Lagon Itol's emergency plan was put into effect. The process to preserve the cultures of the people of Micor began ….

1

The Breadbasket of Bronson Beta

The dark green night sky over Hendron-Khorlu was filled with glowing streaks, heralding Re-Birth Day. These were what was left of Earth, smashed into billion pieces by a collision with Bronson Alpha, one of a pair of stray planets. While the majority of the debris was ejected out into deep space along with the rogue world, drawn by gravity, some of the remnants of the birth place of humanity had remained in orbit, in the form of asteroids, which Bronson Beta, the new and final home of mankind, would pass through annually. It was now a year since the destruction of Earth and the migration of humans to Bronson Beta.

Bronson Beta's year was 205 days long. These were Bronson Beta days, twice as long as Earth's at a smidge over fifty Earth hours. This in effect meant two days' activities in one Bronson Beta day, and thus two "shifts" had evolved: The first of these consisted of a Light Day and a Light Night, during which the Sun still hung in the greenish sky, while the second consisted of a Dark Day, after the Sun had set, and a Dark Night. It was now morning of a Dark Day.

Though the wandering planet had replaced the Earth in its orbit, this was eccentric, taking the alien world almost as close to the Sun as Venus and nearly as far out as Mars. This made for long, cold winters, the first of which was just ending. Spring was coming to Bronson Beta. The Earth colony had proved sustainable, thanks to the domed cities of the Other People, the race that had inhabited the planet before it was flung out into space. It was a time for celebration.

While the survival of humanity was indeed cause for rejoicing, two of the Earth colonists had a more personal reason for celebration. Their child – the first human to be born on Bronson Beta – was soon to arrive.

Tony Drake and his wife Eve Hendron, who was now over six months pregnant, watched the astronomical display overhead, which elicited bittersweet feelings in them. It reminded them that their home world was gone – but also that they had found a *new* home. Their mission had been successful: They had colonized another planet!

Cole Hendron, Eve's father and leader of the League of the Last Days, the organization that had

6

built the two American arks that carried some five hundred people to Bronson Beta, had intended to designate a day of celebration of their safe arrival on the new world. He died before he could do this, as his people made the journey to the city that would come to be named after him. Like Moses, Hendron had laid eyes upon the Promised Land, but did not live to enter it.

A number of problems had naturally enough cropped up after the Americans' arrival, one being the fact that the two arks did not land together. Hendron's keen mind naturally went to solving these problems, putting off any celebration, however well deserved it was. Tony Drake, a tall sandy haired stockbroker and socialite – *former* stockbroker and socialite, as neither stock exchange nor the upper crust of society still existed – had been Hendron's pick to succeed him as leader of the group. With their troubles, which included shelter for the harsh winter, food for the same period and attack by "Asiatics" who had also made it to Bronson Beta, behind them, the young man had declared the anniversary of their arrival as Hendron's planned thanksgiving – Re-Birth Day, when the human race was given a second chance.

Coincidentally, the landing of the arks was very close to the vernal equinox of Bronson Beta, arriving on the night of March 28, 1935. This, it turned out, was four days before spring began, because the axial tilt of the planet did not match Earth's. Doubtless it would settle down, over coming centuries, to match that of the former occupant of the orbit, with the planet tilting away from the Sun at perihelion, and toward it at aphelion. Originally, the refugees had estimated that summer was already in progress when they landed. This turned out to be erroneous, and better calculations followed. They now knew the length of each season.

The timing of Re-Birth Day was fortuitous – Bronson Beta was returning to life after being "dead" for the sixty-eight days of its winter, its surface virtually uninhabitable, and the celebration was therefore twofold.

And not only had the Americans triumphed over all their obstacles, establishing a viable colony, but Tony's bride Eve was pregnant. This announcement had followed their victory over the Asiatic alliance that had menaced them from almost the day they'd arrived. Theirs would be the first child born on this second Earth.

Tony had known Eve on Earth for a number of years, had pursued her, and finally won her over, beating out the hero of the League of the Last Days, Dave Ransdell, a former Great War pilot and commander of the second American ark, the *Mayflower II*. Eve had never loved Ransdell, whom Tony had liked until he'd learned of Eve Hendron's feelings -- that moral obligation might outweigh her personal feelings for Tony, and she might not marry him, despite their three-year relationship prior to the news of impending doom. She was looking at the prospect of rebuilding the human race, not romantic love.

He hadn't given up. Tony Drake was a fighter. He came from a long line of fighters. A Drake had fought in every American war, from the

Revolutionary War to the Great War. The young stockbroker believed that his victory over Ransdell was due in some part to him being named as Cole Hendron's successor – Eve had been very close to her father. Tony didn't care – he loved Eve, and he knew that she loved him. That was all that mattered.

Tony couldn't help but smile as he glanced at his wife, who was watching the meteorites overhead. She was glowing, as pregnant women were often described, under the luminous streaks in the sky. They looked like a fireworks display.

The show was bittersweet. This passage of the planet through the meteroid cloud would wipe out most of the smaller debris. Each year, the annual display would become less and less spectacular as more and more of the meteorites were consumed in Bronson Beta's atmosphere.

The pair was in Hendron-Khorlu, the original home of the Americans before the attack of the Asiatic "Midianites", for a second honeymoon. They had not taken a real one, being busy with establishing society in the domed city of the Other People. They'd had no official ceremony – there was no one to marry them, and, with the imbalance of men to women, many men might have multiple wives. The pair had decided one day that they were now married, so they were.

"Oh, it's beautiful, Tony," Eve breathed.

Catching her husband's gaze out of the corner of a dark eye, the copper-haired woman turned to him, and returned his smile. "What are you grinning about?"

"I was just thinking how lucky we are ... after everything that's happened in the last four years."

After a moment, Eve's smile disappeared. "How do you feel about Nicole?"

"Nicole?" Tony echoed, his wife's somber face alarming him slightly, combined with an unfamiliar name. He couldn't recall any Nicole in the group, though he didn't yet know all of the British newcomers or the Asiatics – actually Russians, Germans and Japanese – who had also joined the Americans, swelling their ranks to more than a thousand. There were hundreds of the latter, and only a fraction of those were irredeemable, having to be exiled. The remainder had been invited to stay, and for the most part, assimilated without trouble.

"I've been trying to find a way to feminize Dad's name and Nicole has been the only thing I could come up with," the copper-haired young woman explained.

Tony knew that she wanted to name a boy Cole after her father, but this was the first he was hearing of a name if their baby was a girl.

"Does that mean ...?"

Eve smiled as she nodded. "Yes. Dr. Osiecki told me just before we left Olympus-Gorfulu." Micorian technology was advanced enough that the gender of fetuses could be determined.

"Oh," Tony grinned. It was a boyish smile, full and unrestrained. He was going to have a daughter! "I suppose Nicole's okay then."

"Okay?" Eve asked in a concerned tone.

"Okay with me," Tony clarified with a grin. Eve Hendron seemed set on naming their child after her father, and Tony did not object, although he might have preferred a name from his own family, or something altogether new, to represent their new life on Bronson Beta, for all life on the planet was new. He might not object too strongly to Antonia, even.

Eve Hendron smiled at her husband's acceptance of her idea, and threw her arms around him.

John Keppler was glad to be home – Hendron-Khorlu, which was inhabited by only a few dozen people. The majority of these were the twenty individuals who had manned the Farm. Among these were Peter and Mary Kenton, a married couple who were husbandry experts. They were the only married couple among the Americans to make the journey to Bronson Beta, and had taken in the Brewster children, Dan, now five years old, and his sister Dorothy, now six. They'd been abandoned near Hendronville, the camp of the League of the Last Days in Michigan, their father hoping they would be shown mercy and taken along on the ark. They were. The two children loved living with the animals in the city.

Originally, a farm had been set up in a river valley a few miles south of where the smaller of the two American arks, named *Noah's Ark*, had landed. Several weeks later, when everyone moved to the safety of the domed city they named Hendron in tribute to the efforts of their leader who had just died, the farm was moved, as well. While humans could survive the long, harsh winter, living inside the cannibalized remains of the ark, the livestock could not, nor could *any* animal that lived outdoors. Hendron-Khorlu had become the agricultural center of the human settlement, which had spread unevenly to the five domed cities – the breadbasket of Bronson Beta.

The livestock they'd brought – cows, horses, sheep and goats; even some reindeer – grazed outside the dome during the warm months, which was about half the year. Silage was put up to feed the animals through the winter. This left the grassy areas of Hendron – small parks and a sports field of some sort – for fruit and the like to be grown year round, their sunlight and moisture carefully maintained by the climate controls of the city via eight great air conditioners, each located near one of the city gates. Fresh fruits and vegetables were a delicacy throughout the winter.

The Earthmen's diet consisted largely of a native grain, which had been stored beneath the city by the original inhabitants, for reasons that were not fully known, supplemented by Earth grains, vegetables and fruits. Meat was a rarity, because so few animals had been brought, even combining that of the four arks. Eventually, if the livestock thrived, it would become as plentiful and common as it had been on Earth. Earth grains and vegetables, put up from the previous year's harvest supplemented the human diet, which was a mixture of Earth and Micorian cuisine.

Keppler was glad to be back to his bees. An entomologist, he was placed in charge of insects necessary for the cultivation of Earth plant life, which included bees, ants, moths, butterflies, locusts and flies. He worked closely with Edgar Higgins, a botanist who oversaw cultivation of plants.

John Keppler wasn't particularly interested in agriculture, except how it involved his precious insects. He had just returned from a trip to the equator, some 2500 miles to the north, where he had established new colonies of bees and ants and others, just south of the formidable Barrier Peaks, so named because they were impassable on foot. While the temperature was pleasant enough now, it would become too hot for human habitation by the summer solstice. The scientist expected that his insects would flourish there, eventually inhabiting every temperate and tropical zone of Bronson Beta. While this latitude was pleasant enough for half the year, the bees couldn't survive the long winter unprotected. The ants might, for the ground of Bronson Beta was heated from below, by residual heat from a radioactive core; the radiation itself did not reach the surface. Keppler planned to start an exterior colony soon, giving the ants time to dig and build before winter came again. Then, he expected, they would thrive as they had on Earth.

The geography of Beta Bronson consisted of four continents, two of which were joined by a prominent archipelago. These were separated from the larger one where Olympus-Gorfulu was located by the small Middle Sea. The pair had been dubbed Borealis, which meant "northern", by Pierre Duquesne, and Australis, which meant "southern"; the southernmost of these two continents possessed a second archipelago to its south that ran almost to the Antarctic Circle. The North Pole was covered by a vast landmass, Polus, most of which was permanently frozen. The southern polar region was also covered by ice, even in summer, and if there was land beneath it, no one knew it.

The four arks – two American, one British and one Asiatic – had all landed on the same massive continent, because it had faced the Earth when the vessels launched. No one had yet named it. It was simply "here". The landmass was roughly an oval, some two thousand miles broad at its narrowest point and seven thousand wide, with a large, irregular peninsula at the northeast that went up very close to the Arctic Circle. The peninsula lay beyond the Barrier Peaks, just south of the equator. The five domed cities were located about halfway along the eastern coast of the super continent at about forty-five degrees latitude.

Pierre Duquesne, the French physicist who had been in charge of building France's ark, had, using only logic, determined that they had landed in the southern hemisphere: Since the season – spring – had remained the same as on Earth, but the planet was now moving in the opposite direction, the hemispheres had to be reversed. He'd turned out to be correct, the night sky proved.

John Keppler's plane landed at Hendron-Khorlu's airfield, and, after being greeted by the staff there – Borden, a meteorologist, made his usual joke, asking about the weather when he knew better than anyone what was going on in the atmosphere of Bronson Beta – the entomologist made his way home, and thence, to his beehives, oblivious to the fact that Re-Birth Day was soon to occur, and most of his fellow residents would go to Olympus-Gorfulu for the celebration. He was more concerned with his bees than the activities of his fellow humans.

2

The City of the Argonauts

It was late May 1936 as preparations for Re-Birth Day began in Olympus-Gorfulu, the capital of the human settlement, but Earth's calendar had been discarded in favor of one more appropriate to mankind's new home. Two hundred and five, the number of days in the Bronson Beta year, did not divide easily. Therefore, the new calendar consisted of five months, each comprised of forty-one days: Unumber, Duober, Tribusber, Quattuorber and Quinqueber, using the Latin method employed to name September, October, November and December. There was no need to give some months more days than others, doing it in this manner, as had occurred on Earth.

16

Unumber began the day of the vernal equinox, which was Re-Birth Day. The holiday had been the deciding factor in beginning the new year on the vernal equinox, rather than the winter solstice: A new year was a form of re-birth in itself, and so Re-Birth Day was the first day of Unumber. The new calendar began with year one, A.E. – After Earth, the last four days of which the refugees of Earth had spent on Bronson Beta. "Weeks" had been kept as colloquial term, referring to seven shifts, each of which resembled an Earth day, rather than to seven Bronson Beta days. There were sixty-one of these in a year, and excluded the beginning-of-year holiday, Re-Birth Day.

One of the proponents of the new calendar had been Pierre Duquesne, a French physicist who had been in charge of building the failed French ark, and who was now a consultant to the Central Authority, a guiding committee that was originally comprised of ten members of the two American arks. With the influx of new citizens, members from the other factions, the British and the "Asiatics", which was a mix, culturally, of Germans, Russians and Japanese, alternations had been made to the make up of the council, so that each group was better represented. The German Innsbruck and the Japanese Hiyakawa had become members, as well as Lady Cynthia Cruikshank and Major Griggsby-Cook, Brits. This came as close to an accurate repsentation of the populcare as could be had.

The Frenchman worked closely with Jessup and Kane, two scientists who were in charge of analyzing Micorian technology. They had been the true minds behind the second ark, with Dave Ransdell only nominally in charge as flight commander.

Duquesne now spoke with Professor Lawrence Philbin, who was a linguist that had been instrumental in understanding the language of the natives of Bronson Beta. Both were small men, and they sat in large chairs that faced one another, with a small table upon which a board game rested between them. This entertainment, Calmat, had belonged to the natives of Bronson Beta, and had become quite popular among humans.

Duquesne was something of a philosopher, in addition to being a physicist. No one knew if he was this way before the arrival of the twin planets, Bronson Alpha and Bronson Beta, but he certainly was one now. He liked to speculate about the original inhabitants of Bronson Beta, the Micorites, as they were called, although the study of culture was not his specialty.

Philbin, who had begun the long process of translating Micorian records, was a natural conversational companion for the Frenchman. There probably wasn't anyone in the city more knowledgeable about the former inhabitants of the planet than Philbin, due to his translation of Micorian texts, and so, naturally, Duquesne enjoyed speaking to him about this subject. What had become of the original inhabitants of Bronson Beta was a frequent topic between the two men.

"I have decided," pronounced Duquesne as he scratched his protruding belly, "that the granaries were intended to sustain the Other People in the event that the orbit of Micor shifted due to the passage of Borak."

"Oh?" said Philbin. It was the first time that he had heard this particular theory. Beneath each of the five domed cities there lay a vast granary, each of which would keep the human population fed for their lifetimes and beyond.

"What other possible explanation? The Micorites" – this was a term Duquesne himself had coined, as he had a number of others – "could not possibly hope to survive a voyage through space such as Bronson Beta took, with the surface frozen over as it was. If we lived on Mars, or on Venus, we might have taken similar precautions, like the ancient peoples of Earth did, as security against famine and drought. They hoped that the perturbance would be slight, and that their planet would continue in a stable orbit, even if it was not exactly as it had been before the arrival of Borak."

"Hmmm," Philbin mused as he moved one of the pieces on the board. These were colored red and gold, and, like chess pieces, did not bear much resemblance to anything in reality. Whether this was because they had no such basis, or because they were meant to be an abstract, artful form, no one could be sure. The game was ancient, its origins lost to time. There was variety in the various sets of the game to be found, differing styles. This had fed a number of conversations between the two men, Philbin taking the view that the natives were more spiritually enlightened than humans. He drew this conclusion from their art, as well as their writings he had deciphered.

"In essence," Duquesne continued as he took his turn – the goal of the game was to move pieces across the board without having them captured or trapped – "that is what we humans did – except we relocated to another world. We brought our granaries with us, hoping that Bronson Beta would assume a stable orbit that would prove viable for our colony to survive."

"You might be onto something," Philbin admitted. He glanced up as his conversational partner's common law wife, Marlene Dietrich, entered the room, carrying a tray of what passed for tea on Bronson Beta. This was brewed from a native plant, and while not exactly like tea, made for a passable substitute.

The German actress and Duquesne had become acquainted when they lived next door to one another in Hendron-Khorlu. How she had come to be in Hendronville, the camp on Earth that built the American arks, Philbin did not know. But since arriving on Bronson Beta, she had devoted herself to creating a theater company, which had become quite popular. Perching herself on the arm of her husband's chair, the trim blonde actress smiled at Duquesne, obviously enamored of him. She was quite fascinated by his brilliant mind. "Are you winning, dahling?" she asked.

"Of course he's winning," Philbin answered, rather tartly. He didn't care for the interruption to his concentration, either in the game or the conversation. He ignored Marlene as she poured the "tea" into cups and distributed them.

"The only remaining question is, what happened to the corpses?" continued the French physicist, picking up his own cup and sipping at the hot brew. It was aromatic, with an odor all its own, unlike anything on Earth. It was not altogether unpleasant, especially when flavored with honey from Keppler's bees.

Duquesne was a staunch coffee man, but, as yet, no suitable substitute had been found. Higgins was still tinkering with his coffee plants, and they had not yet produced a viable crop of beans. "Someone had to be last, in case of mercy killing or mass suicide." This, too, had been a frequent topic of discussion among the Earth people when they had first discovered the domed cities completely empty.

"I think I've got that one solved," announced the linguist. He glanced up at Duquesne to see the Frenchman waiting with bated breath. "They went outside to die quickly."

"Oh, ho!" puffed the physicist. He tugged at his black beard, an indication that he was thinking deeply.

"When they saw that they were doomed, that their preparations had failed," explained Philbin, "they all left the protection of the domes and died outside."

"Why have we not found any corpses then?" Duquesne challenged, his black-as-coal eyes fiery.

"They decomposed before Bronson Beta froze. Or their bodies were destroyed by natural catastrophes like those that racked Earth on the Bronson planets' first pass through the Solar System."

21

The Frenchman leaned back in his chair and pondered this theory while Philbin considered his next move.

Dave Ransdell had left Olympus-Gorfulu several days earlier, when the weather began to improve, leaving his seat in Central Authority vacant. He had been in charge of security.

There was no need for a standing army: All able-bodied men were considered to be reservists, though since the fall of Midian, the domed city inhabited by the Asiatic alliance that had been nicknamed after the oppressors of the Israelites in the Old Testament, no further threats had emerged. But someone had been needed when the position was created, and there were still civil disputes to mediate.

Dave had nominated Peter Vanderbilt to replace him. Peter was no longer a young man, now in his early forties, and fearless. Though he was a Fifth Avenue New Yorker, he was not an ineffectual upper crust effete. He had proven his courage most recently by leading a raid into Midian – what was now called Olympus-Gorfulu – to set in motion the fall of the Asiatic "Midianites". His small commando team of five had been greatly aided, without their knowledge, by Marian Jackson, a very brave young woman who had been a stowaway on the second of the American arks. When the Midianite camp had been thrown into chaos after Marian killed their leader, Seidel, Peter and his men had rallied the captive Brits to overthrow the Asiatics.

22

Tony Drake had no problem with Peter becoming the new head of security. Peter Vanderbilt was a solidly built fellow of average height, his prematurely graying hair brushed back from his face. It had been kept in place with a gel on Earth. On Bronson Beta, the New Yorker had found a suitable substitute among the Micorites' many concoctions. The two men had known one another on Earth: Tony's mother had gone to school with Peter's older sister.

Peter Vanderbilt quickly enlisted a handful of men he could rely upon: Jack Little, Tony's club friend who had been on the second ark with Dave Ransdell; Bill Whittington, who had proven himself in the raid on Midian; Eric Leeds, one of the Brits. He'd been in the British Army, the only one of the quartet with military experience. These four acted as the police force of Olympus-Gorfulu, and they were not busy. Those chosen to journey to the new Earth – at least in the American camp – had been picked for their superior intellectual and emotional qualities. There were no troublemakers in the city, though, occasionally, some residents got into trouble. The small police force did not even go about armed, all firearms in the city being checked into the armory for emergency use only.

The biggest squabbles originated in politics. The Asiatics were socialists, and had been forced to foreswear proselytizing in exchange for being allowed to join the common community. Those that didn't – there were about twenty of these – were exiled. Generally, the threat of banishment from civilization was enough to curtail the more violent disagreements they were prone to.

Olympus-Gorfulu, though possessing a jail that was run like that of any small town in America, did not have a true prison, meant for long-tern punishment. What the Micorites had done to their criminals was still unknown.

Occasionally, race was the motive for altercations. The city was now inhabited by a diverse group, Americans – who were of various ethnic backgrounds, and some of whom were Negroes – Brits, Germans, Russians and Japanese. Even the odd Frenchman or German.

The reasons for these outbreaks usually came down to one thing: *klul*, an intoxicating gas invented by the Micorites, used as alcohol had been used on Earth.

Not that Bronson Beta was liquor-less. A small group of enterprising young men had gone into the moonshine racket, using the native grain of the planet. They called their product Bronson's White Lightning, the company logo being a white lightning bolt superimposed on a green globe. They did a rather brisk business, being the only manufacturer in town, so to speak.

A young red-haired man entered the security office. "*Hopayiato*," he said to Peter. In Micorese, this meant something like "How the devil are you?" Snatches of the native tongue had worked their way into the speech of those in Olympus-Gorfulu, particularly among the young. Practically everyone in the five cities spoke *some* Micorese, which had been learned from the educational machines used in schools to teach Micorian children. Those who did not use the machines picked it up from conversation with those who had.

Seeing the puzzled expression on the pleasant face of Jack Taylor, Peter asked, "What's wrong?"

"Missing hairbrush," answered the redhead. In addition to being a top student at Cornell, he was also an athlete, tall and broad shouldered. He had acquired something of a reputation as a Romeo in Olympus-Gorfulu, the willing prey -- up to a certain point – of several eligible young women. None had yet managed to permanently ensnare him with their charms.

Peter's face mirrored the puzzled expression of Jack's. "I don't understand this. This isn't the first such theft. Why would anyone steal such small, personal items? The machines here can replicate anything anyone would need. I'd guess it was the Asiatics, but this is a workers' paradise. And I can't imagine anyone in our group doing something like this." Cole Hendron had picked the survivors of Earth for their wisdom and morality, in addition to their scientific expertise, to ensure the best possible chance of survival for humanity. That left the British members of the settlers, who had been chosen by lottery, and thereforewere comprised of every type of individual, both good and bad.

"Maybe it's Clara," suggested Jack.

Clara was a monkey that had stowed away on the *Mayflower II*, which had been commanded by Dave Ransdell. No one had claimed ownership of her, or confessed to bringing her aboard. The consensus was that she'd escaped from a nearby zoo.

Even though she was not part of the plan, she was a welcome member of the community. Every other animal brought to Bronson Beta had been chosen for their usefulness, even cats. Humans needed companionship, and cats had been selected over dogs because of their independent nature. There was nothing to hunt, or need protection from, so the dogs' only selling point was their companionship – weighed against the care they required. Cats had won out. All other fauna served as food in one form or another, whether it was eaten or the production of edible goods such as milk or eggs, or used for pollination of edible plants.

"Good idea. I'll look it into it."

"Thanks," Jack replied, grinning sheepishly. Peter suspected one of the young women Jack was seeing had put him up to reporting the "crime", knowing his connection to the New Yorker; both had come over on the second ark, deputies of sorts to Ransdell.

Nodding, Jack departed, leaving Peter to muse about the string of thefts that had occurred over the past couple of weeks.

Eliot James, an Oxford poet who was also a diarist, had become the official historian of the human settlement, as well as the colony's librarian. The final layer of insulation in the original ark had been books – a multitude of them. Humanity's culture had been preserved, and James had become its caretaker – in addition to the works of the Micorites. Not many of these had been borrowed from Olympus-Gorfulu's lending library. Not many were literate enough in Micorese to read it for pleasure. The English section, however, was quite busy, since there was little labor to be done with machines that did most of the work and repaired themselves.

Eliot James looked up from his journal to gaze down at the celebration preparations from his apartment in one of the many towers of Olympus-Gorfulu, the new home of the Earth refugees, then returned to his writing. It said:

> One year. We have been lived on this alien world for one year. One Bronson Beta year, that is, which is 428 Earth days. With winter ending, all doubts of our survival have left us. Beneath each of the five domed cities of the Other People is a granary that will feed our population for centuries. The Central Authority has decided that plants brought from Earth will be cultivated on the land around Hendron-Khorlu, which was turned into a farm when the rest of us re-located to Olympus-Gorfulu, a move dictated by the power to the five cities being generated at and controlled from there.
>
> The capital of the quartet of subsidiary cities was so named in emulation of Hendron-Khorlu; the native name, once learned, was added to the name we had given it. Olympus was chosen, after some debate, because, being the hub of the ring of cities, Gorfulu is the most powerful of them, and capital of the god-

like beings who inhabited Bronson Beta. God-like with respect to technology, at any rate. Though they seem quite enlightened by Earth standards, they likely had their own foibles, which of course were discreetly not recorded in theri history books. Vanity may be a symptom of higher intelligence, no matter where it breeds.

But the name "Olympus" originated because several of us have been referring to ourselves as "Argonauts", the legendary heroes of Greece who undertook a dangerous journey. Our goal was not a golden fleece, but a new home.

The original name of this world, Micor, never caught on the way the others did. Bronson Beta-Micor is just too much of a mouthful, it seems.

Life settled into a routine during the long winter. Exploration of the other cities was undertaken; the most northerly of the five, Strahl, had never been visited by anyone from our group before, and Danot, the city to the east, only briefly by Peter Vanderbilt and his group as they infiltrated Midian – our name for Gorfulu before our capture of it. A few people moved into the other cities, but not many. The domed cities are too much like ghost towns for most of us.

As the temperature increased over the past several days, adventurous souls have made excursions outside of the dome. Travel between the five cities had been confined to use of the underground passages (by which Peter's group had snuck into Midian), and the speedy little cars designed for use in the tunnels. Land around Hendron-Khorlu is being surveyed for spring planting. A new chapter is about to begin on Bronson-Beta.

Doctor Charles Dodson, who had lost his right arm at the camp in Michigan when it was attacked, could no longer practice surgery. But that did not mean that he had given up medicine altogether. If fact, he ran the hospital in Olympus-Gorfulu. Since no bureaucrats had been among the refugees – each possessed a skill of some sort necessary to rebuilding civilization, and pushing papers was not considered an essential one – he served as chief of medicine and head of operations of the hospital, as well, leaving surgical operations to Dr. Alan Smith. Dodson had been third on Hendron's list to make the journey to Bronson Beta, and also served on the Central Authority, in charge of policies.

Fortunately, he was not the only doctor among those who had come to Bronson Beta. There were a number among the British and Asiatics, as well. These days, the hospital's main business consisted of examining and counseling pregnant women in the city. There were, in fact, a number of young men and women trained in this specialty, since populating the new Earth was the secondary duty of everyone who had come across, the first being establishing the basic foundation of a sustainable physical camp.

Obstetrics was a booming business, now that life on Bronson Beta had settled down into routine that people felt comfortable conceiving children. Many common-law marriages had formed in the months since settling in Olympus-Gorfulu, and somewhere near fifty couples were expecting their first child.

Dodson happened to be in the hospital when a number of unconscious men were brought in. Normally, the small hospital did not see such a rush, as injuries and illnesses were few and far between. In fact, he recalled only one time when a number of people had required medical treatment all at once. Shortly after the Americans' arrival in Bronson Beta, more than two dozen had fallen unconscious. Lucy Grant, Bates, an engineer, and Wardlow, a chemist, never awoke.

Since the camp had been attacked not much later by the Asiatics, it was widely believed that they were responsible for the deaths, the exact cause of which had never been determined. It was known that the others used a gas developed by the natives of Bronson Beta, and this had been blamed.

As Dodson hurried to the intake room, he heard one of his staff, a young intern by the name of Dolan, exclaim, "It's the Sleeping Sickness again! They've got it!"

3

A Titan of New Earth

Dave Ransdell's mission as he flew his crimson-colored lark west largely consisted of map making. Very little of Bronson Beta had been mapped as it neared Earth, because it was a hunk of ice until it had rounded the Sun once and begun to thaw. It had passed close enough to the blazing orb that millennia of ice evaporated over the course of two years – helped by a radioactive core that kept the planet from completely freezing – and plant life had begun to bloom after a million years of hibernation. Astronomers had then gotten a decent peek at this section of the planet, the one that faced Earth as it approached. Remnants of cities had been sighted, the five domed cities now claimed by humans. But there was still so much unknown about this massive continent upon which humans had settled, which was larger than Eurasia. This had given the South African explorer a plausible reason to leave Olympus-Gorfulu, one that was not *entirely* false.

A restless, adventuring soul was one thing that had impelled Dave to leave Olympus-Gorfulu as soon as weather permitted. The nighttime temperature at the latitude of the city during winter was 35 below zero Fahrenheit, which prohibited travel out into the wilds of Bronson Beta as the South African desired. There was no chance of survival if something went wrong with his little plane. The roads were buried in snow for the duration of winter, and went unused during that season. Instead, travelers moved about underground: Tunnels connected the five cities, and these were used by those wishing to travel between cities. Dave was one of these who explored the other cities in the grouping of five, early in the settlement of Olympus-Gorfulu. He spent little time in that city after its conquest, if it could be called that. "Civil war" might be a better term for what had occurred, or "revolution". "Slave revolt" might describe it best, as the British prisoners overthrew their jailers.

Dave Ransdell had been viewed by many as Cole Hendron's natural successor: He possessed the same magnetic personality and was a natural leader. But Tony Drake's assistance to Hendron in the early days after landing had given him the edge, while Ransdell was leading the second, larger ark, some miles to the south, unknown to either party. Dave didn't harbor any ill feelings toward Tony, who was well qualified to succeed Hendron. As fit as he was to lead, the South African was something of a loner.

What stung more was his loss of Eve to Tony. It was perfectly understandable, her choosing Tony over Dave. He was young, closer to Eve's age than his own, and they had a shared history on Earth before the Bronson bodies arrived. And her father had made his own choice clear. Probably, their relationship had been cemented by the sixty days they'd shared before the people of the two arks found each other.

Fulfilling his lust for adventure helped Dave ease the pain of these twin losses. He was the type to take such setbacks in stride, and not dwell upon them. In certain ways, he was a remarkable figure.

Dave Ransdell could have been the protagonist in a pulp novel. He was big and blond, possessing Herculean strength in his mighty frame. Though passionate about the things he believed in, he was close-mouthed, preferring to listen rather than to speak. He lived by Plato's dictum: "Wise men speak because they have something to say; fools because they have to say something." Dave spoke when necessary, and not needlessly. Which was not to say that he was a somber fellow. He was not. He was good natured, if possessing a subdued sense of humor born out of a childhood of hard work.

Dave was famous on Earth, before the end, for discovering a new metal brought up from the depths of the planet by the first passage of the twin rogue planets, three years after they had first been sighted. The Earth's crust had been rent asunder in a number of places, revealing new elements even as the disturbance killed millions. This hitherto unknown substance had been used to construct the tubes of the atomic motors of the American arks, which had to endure unearthly heat; no other metal known on Earth was capable of such a feat. It had been named Ransdellium after him.

But in his homeland of the Union of South Africa, Dave Ransdell had been a hero long before the arrival of the Bronson planets. He had been the first Ransdell to be born in South Africa. His father, an Englishman, had married a young woman from Montana and took her to the Transvaal where he sought his fortune by mining diamonds. Dave had been born in Pretoria soon after.

When the Great War started, the Union of South Africa was relatively new nation; its name reflected its origin uniting four formerly separate British colonies. Dutch had been the primary language of the region, due to the Dutch East India Company's colonization of the area in the 1600s, at what would become Cape Town, then became heavily-accented English when Great Britain acquired the region in 1795 in order to keep the French from taking control of it when they invaded the Dutch Republic. The British expanded their control in the late nineteenth century through a series of wars with the native Zulu and the Boers, Dutch settlers who had left the area because of British rule and settled elsewhere, forming the Boer republics. Finally, the Union of South Africa was created as a dominion of the British Empire in 1910, joining the territories of the Natal and Cape colonies and the republics of the Orange Free State and the Transvaal, which was the home of the Ransdell family.

In 1897, when Dave was born, the Transvaal was an independent country known as the South African Republic – "Zuid-Afrikaansche Republiek" in Dutch, the tongue of the settlers. Z.A.R., the acronym of the country's name in that language, was a popular term among citizens. It had defeated the British in the First Boer War, but had lost the second, losing its independence when it was forced to surrender in 1902. The British changed the name of the former nation to the Transvaal Colony, Transvaal being a local name indicating its location north of the Vaal River. This move was made to wipe away the cultural identity of the mostly Dutch residents of the area, and almost everyone took it hard.

Dave Ransdell was like his father, an adventurous, restless soul. It ran in the family. So young Dave, being a Ransdell, jumped at the chance to fight in the Great War, leaving school to do so. Still a teenager when the conflict started in 1914, he was still naïve and held romantic ideals about war. He didn't understand that war was dirty business. But he learned. He learned in the skies over France as a pilot, where the chivalry imagined by civilians disappeared early in the war.

When Great Britain declared war on Germany, South Africa naturally joined in, releasing British soldiers there to join the fight, as well as forming their own plans to invade German South-West Africa, which they successfully did, as well as doing the same to German East Africa.

Dave, wanting to be a pilot, served in Europe. He had been shot down twice, narrowly escaping death both times, but had succeeded in becoming a multiple ace before the war was over. An ace had to shoot down five enemy planes. Before armistice was declared, Dave had shot down twenty-five, one short of the Allied powers' record.

He returned home but could muster no enthusiasm for continuing the pedestrian work of the small ranch and mining operation that his father had begun before Dave had been born. It was successful enough to allow him to raise a family, as his father had, but he had no interest in that. Not after the death he'd seen during the war. Transvaal now seemed too small for him, and he longed for bigger things.

Dave spent most of the next decade flying mail routes in southern Africa, and he managed to get in some exploration, as well, mapping unknown regions of the Dark Continent. He was enjoying his vagabond life.

Then had come the Bronson planets and the world changed for everyone.

Once the weather on Bronson Beta had begun to turn fair once more, Dave Ransdell had taken his "lark", the native plane that was named for the Earth bird which it resembled, west to an unexplored region of the continent. This land mass was two thousand miles broad and seven thousand miles wide. Only a fraction had been surveyed, the area around the five cities. No one really had any idea what lay beyond them. And this was but one of four continents. There was an entire world to explore, and Dave intended on seeing as much of it as possible before he died.

Flying to the west coast, as Dave intended, would not take long. The little larks, powered by alien technology, flew at 350 miles per hour. One could fly from coast to coast and back again in one Bronson Beta day. But that wasn't his goal, merely traversing the massive continent's width. The explorer wanted to explore. He had mapped about one thousand miles both north and south of the latitude line, which was about 45 degrees, where Olympus-Gorfulu was situated as he flew west. He'd found that a mountain range spanned the continent, running from the southeast to the northwest, virtually dividing the continent in half.

He was surprised to find another grouping of five domed cities, or at least one of them, and one of the metallic roads from it leading south indicating that there were others, as in the east. Dave and the other Earthmen were under the impression that the quintet they knew was the only such place. There could be dozens of such arrangements on the planet, which was nearly identical in size to Earth, he realized. But he didn't stop to explore it, as it appeared identical to the domed cities he knew.

The South African explorer had stopped earlier when he'd sighted ruins of ancient cities, obliterated by the tremendous force that pushed Bronson Beta out of orbit, but nothing useful had been left behind. The only recognizable structures visible from the air were megaliths that vaguely resembled the pyramids in Egypt. These, however, were three-sided, and probably at one time near-perfect tetrahedrons. They would become archaeological digs when Dave returned to Olympus-Gorfulu and told everyone about them.

When he encountered a second, minor mountain range, Dave followed that south a ways, until it petered out, before turning west again. The west was more mountainous than the east, which held a range in the middle latitudes, where the arks had landed, and another, longer one in the south. These, Dave had learned, were part of the same continent-spanning range.

Both ends of the continent contained many rivers, and Dave wondered how many had been formed as a result of the great thaw that had just occurred.

It was chiller here than in the east. The cold waters of the South Sea and the antarctic winds made this an alpine climate, as opposed to Olympus-Gorfulu's temperate clime. The trees here reflected this. Suited for cold weather, they were closer to Earth's coniferous trees than deciduous.

Dave had many days' supplies of food and water with him, and was in no hurry to return to Olympus-Gorfulu. He stopped from time to time to refill his water cans at lakes that were reminders of the planet's recent frozen past. These were, in effect, glacial tarns. He never saw any sign of the civilization that had existed a million years earlier, except in the form of domed cities and mystery megaliths, the latter of which he might have mistaken for natural formations if he'd hadn't been looking for them.

38

After several days, Dave finally reached the west coast. Turning his lark northward, he followed the coastline. The jagged edge of this bespoke of volcanic activity such had been visited upon the Earth by the presence of the Bronson twins. This idea was soon confirmed when Dave spotted the remains of an ancient city, fallen into the sea.

He circled his lark around the site, fascinated by what he saw.

Not much of the domed city was still visible. The dome had broken, a sliver of it jutting up from the green surf, just breaking the surface. The light from the nightly aurora glinted off it. Otherwise, Dave would have missed it.

The road above ended at a cliff. Everything else had been swallowed by the sea. The explorer guessed that this had occurred when Borak drew near, some million years earlier, and not recently. Bronson Beta had not come near enough Earth for one planet to affect the other. It was Bronson Alpha that was the planet killer.

Dave gazed out the transparent metal of the cockpit of the lark, his blue eyes following the broken road. This shone like a silver ribbon in the starlight of Dark Day. Brilliant hues coruscated off it like oil on water, creating a weird rainbow effect. The road led east, undoubtedly toward the remainder of a set of five cities, one of which he had probably spied previously – he'd have to check his maps to be certain. The continent was a big place and there might even be more than two sets of five cities.

Dave was tempted to follow the road, to confirm his belief, but decided against it. He had plotted the city he'd seen on his map, and he could re-visit it if he chose. Since there were no roads between the quintets of domed metropolises, finding them by air would be the only way to do so. The fact that the only roads they'd found in the east led from one of those five to another in the group seemingly confirmed the belief that there were no other cities on Bronson Beta.

Dave imagined the expeditions that would follow when he relayed the news of this second quintet. Was the west a separate nation? How did its culture differ from what they had learned from the Five Cities? He would leave that to the scientists among the colonists, Philbin and Jessup and Kane and others.

Dave took his plane down toward the sunken city for a closer look, fascinated by what he saw. He somehow expected better of the Micorites – their technology was so advanced, he didn't think they should have been surprised by the seismic disturbances caused by the approach of Borak. Earth scientists expected it as the Bronson twins arrived – but were powerless to stop them. The coastlines of every continent had been swallowed by the sea, destroying every city, town and village on shores. Millions died in the first pass of the two planets – fully half of Earth's population.

As the lark descended so that its pilot could get a better look at the sunken city, unusual movement in the water caught Dave's attention. Something was moving under the water!

4

What Lies Beneath

Dave Ransdell directed the lark out over the turbulent waters of Oceanus, which was just as green as the eastern Middle Sea was. This body of water was expansive, some six thousand miles from shore to shore – this from the observations made from Earth. Bronson Beta had not yet been srurveyed to improve such estimates. That was part of Dave's mapping mission.

From his altitude, he couldn't make out what was moving in the water, and descended to find out. He expected to find a machine that had survived the cataclysm of its home city below. Perhaps, being situated on the coast, the inhabitants had built boats, or even submarines!

The camp living in Olympus-Gorfulu had not yet adapted Micorian technology for sea travel – there'd been no reason to do so. Planes and cars got them everywhere they needed to go. There was no pressing need to fly to other lands, though this would undoubtedly come with time.

Yes, Dave observed – there was definitely something moving under the surface. It appeared large, based on the disturbance it was causing, but he couldn't see anything. The seawater was opaque, hiding whatever lay hidden beneath the surface. From what he saw, this ocean was much more turbulent than the semi-enclosed Middle Sea.

Dave took the ship down, nearly skimming the surface. Peering through the transparent metal of the canopy, his eyes roved the sea.

Suddenly, a giant sea serpent lurched from the surf!

The explorer jerked back on the controls, sending the lark up into the sky. The huge teeth of the gargantuan monstrosity nipped at the little red plane.

Dave watched as the creature breached and fell back into the water like a whale. He saw that it was not a serpent at all, merely a very long – and very large – fish-like creature. It possessed a long face in which two rows of sharp teeth sat. Its neck was very long, like that of a giraffe, its body squat like that of a turtle. It disappeared beneath the surf.

Dave watched as the thing followed him – he couldn't see the body but he saw the disturbance it left on the surface as it swam – its head remained near the surface. It was incredibly fast. Not as fast as the lark, of course, but fast. It could overtake an Earth speedboat, the South African estimated.

The explorer took the ship down for a closer look – not too close, of course. He had a good idea of the thing's size and how far it could leap, and kept well out of its range as he brought the lark around and circled over the creature.

It reared up again, coming up out of the water. It was a magnificent creature. Dave wished he had a camera, and, although some had been brought from Earth, he had not expected to see anything worth photographing. Now, he thought he would never see anything on Bronson Beta more worth photographing!

The weird creature dropped back into the water, belly flopping, which sent a geyser up into the air nearly as high as the lark flew.

Perhaps they'd name it after him, Dave thought with a wan smile playing at his lips. He'd already been honored in that way once – for his discovery of the new heavy metal brought up from beneath Earth's crust by the volcanic activity by the passing of the two Bronson planets – Ransdellium. Perhaps they'd call this creature a "Ransdellosaurus".

The notion amused him, and no more. Dave Ransdell had no interest in such honors.

The thought of volcanic activity made the South African explorer recall what Higgins had discovered: It was still warm beneath the surface of Bronson Beta, because, he'd deduced, of radioactivity that heated the crust. The rocky layer blocked the radiation from reaching the surface, but retained the heat of it. The same thing had to have occurred in the oceans: While the surface had frozen over, water remained a liquid near the ocean floor, warm enough to support life – and enough of it to feed giant creatures like the Ransdellosaurus. Who knew how many other kinds of sea creatures existed, hidden by the green water of the Bronson Beta seas?

The long-necked beast broke the surface once again, its crocodile-like jaws snapping at the lark as it passed overhead – but Dave didn't bring the ship down any lower than one hundred feet.

Finally, the Ransdellosaurus gave up and swam away. Dave followed it with his eyes, watching it head out to sea, then, he pointed his plane north.

After an hour of flying, he saw something out of the ordinary. It wasn't something left behind by the original inhabitants of Bronson Beta – it was too small to be a city, too big to be a vehicle. But it was definitely metallic – the Dark Day starlight glinted off of it.

Then, suddenly, Dave Ransdell realized what it was – it was another ark from Earth!

5

The Long Winter of Nova Italia

Dave Ransdell circled the site, and saw why the ark was not immediately recognizable: It was no longer a long cylindrical shape, but had been cannibalized to make a self-contained habitat. This was comprised of a number of squat cylindrical buildings that used to be the middle section of the ship connected by smaller hemispherical tubes. Whoever had designed it, it was much more self-sufficient than the arks of the Americans, British and Asiatics. Everyone else had counted on Bronson Beta being habitable. This looked more like something one might put on the Moon, something designed for long-term habitation in a hostile environment.

Still, they couldn't have brought enough food to last much longer than had already passed, some four hundred and thirty Earth days. Of course, that depended on the original size of the ship, and the number of passengers. Each of the other arks had carried more than two hundred people, some much more. Judging by the size of the buildings, Dave guessed that might be about right.

Bringing the lark in low, he buzzed the place, hoping to alert any below to his presence. By all appearances, the habitat could be uninhabited. No lights were visible and no one was in sight, and the shiny metal surface of the buildings was gone, wiped away by the long winter of Bronson Beta. Still, it was too cold to be out long in the darkness, even though spring was near. Someone might be inside.

Numerous wooden structures had been constructed, the purpose of which was not immediately obvious in Dave's flyovers; the area, the explorer saw, had been cleared of timber. This seemed to fuel the dual purposes of providing a suitable area for assembly of the habitat and providing fresh lumber for construction. The work that had been done was quite impressive. Whoever lived below were an industrious people.

As he flew over it, Dave pondered the state of the site. The American arks had been abandoned when a domed city was found. Perhaps whoever traveled in this ark had done the same.

Now Dave wished he'd stopped at the domed city he spied to the east. Based on the city that had fallen into the sea, the one inland had been the northerly one of the quintet. Perhaps the passengers of the ark below had made it there; perhaps not.

No road led to it from the shoreline here. A road discovered at the landing site in the east had led to exploration by the American camp. They'd been fortunate enough to land near the one leading from Danot, north of the camp, to Khorlu in the south. If Khorlu was Washington, D.C. – as it had been in Tony Drake's explanation of the geography he'd covered in his exploratory flight – then Danot was somewhere in New Hampshire.

Before he could ponder this possibility further, Dave saw a man below – then another. Soon, a small army poured out of the habitat. They were bundled up in winter clothing.

Suddenly, floodlights filled the night, illuminating the area around the converted ark.

The South African took the lark back up to find a suitable landing spot, and when he found one a few minutes later, brought the small ship in for a perfect landing. He was as good a pilot as had existed on Earth, and certainly the best on Bronson Beta. He had also logged the most hours on the Micorian planes.

Men and women, dressed in little more than rags, swarmed the lark as it rolled to a stop. Their faces were emaciated, Dave noticed, though not badly so. Without the benefit of the technology of the Micorites, their lives had been hard. Probably, their food supplies were running low. Well, he could tell them about the edible plants on Bronson Beta.

But another thought was foremost in his mind: Perhaps they could be asked to join the others in

Olympus-Gorfulu. There was more than enough room for them in the Five Cities, and more than enough food.

Their appearances reminded Dave of the Asiatic exiles: Those twenty who had been judged to be irredeemable had been banished to the Colony. This was the site of the farm, which was located in a valley a few miles south of the landing site of the first, smaller American vessel, dubbed *Noah's Ark*. Earth plants had been cultivated there, before the discovery of the domed cities. Coincidentally, twenty people had operated it. The two arks had been cannibalized in much the same way this one had been, and converted into a self-sufficient habitat for the exiles. Too small for the full complement of Earthmen, it was quite roomy for twenty.

There had been some argument over this solution. Eliot James was against it, suggesting instead the Asiatic renegades be sent to one of the other domed cities, but was opposed by those who felt that this was too dangerous: Giving them access to the advanced technology of the Micorites, even in one of the satellite cities, was potentially catastrophic. The machines and devices there could be used as weapons, or to make weapons. This opinion had carried the day, and the irredeemables were sent to the Colony. They had been given food to sustain them for the winter, but were expected to do their own farming during the summer, and to store enough food for the coming winter. The land was good and a fresh water river ran through the valley. There was plenty of timber nearby to fuel fires to keep the residents warm, in case of a problem with their electric heaters. It would be hard work, but the Colony could be self-sufficient. Meat was delivered to them in rations, carefully controlled as it was among the Argonauts themselves.

Of course, the exiles were free to leave the Colony. But there was no place else to go, really. The dome gates were now manned to prevent outsiders from getting in, so if those renegades left the Colony, they would have to start completely over.

Unsurprisingly, those banished there called the Colony "Siberia", which was known for its gulags, or prison camps. Stalin's political enemies had been sent there. In this respect, the Colony *was* Siberia – those sent there were sent for political reasons – they were anarchists, revolutionaries and rabble rousers. Troublemakers with a capital "T".

In their early days on Bronson Beta, those in the American camp had spoken about migrating closer to the equator, where the winter temperatures would not be fatal. However, the summer temperatures would be, unless the colony moved underground. Thankfully, the discovery of the domed cities of the Other People stopped this plan from becoming a necessity.

A miasma of words bombarded Dave as he opened the canopy of the crimson lark. These were spoken loudly, quickly – urgently, excitedly. Through the cacophony, he recognized that they were Italian.

Of course! It was believed the Italians had been working on an ark themselves, but this had never been confirmed in the chaos and confusion of the final days on Earth – *of* Earth. Such projects had often remained secret, in order to stop the public from mobbing construction sites, demanding to be taken aboard the ships. This very thing had occurred in Michigan, five months before the end.

Dave Ransdell was mobbed as he exited the lark, drawing his big frame from the compartment. He spoke loudly, in order to be heard over the multitude of voices. Finally, someone answered in English. This was heavily accented but understandable.

"American?" the voice asked.

"That's right," Dave nodded, stepping down off the wing.

"Where is your camp?"

"East ... a few thousand miles," the explorer explained. "These planes are quite fast."

The dark eyes of the speaker – a swarthy, black-haired fellow – went to the lark. He said something in Italian to his fellow refugees, and a conversation broke out among them.

Finally, in English, he asked Dave, "Did you bring this from Earth? None of us have seen anything like it before." The lark was a compact little ship, powerful. It was powered by a force or means unknown on Earth, a blend of electrical impulses and radioactivity. Even now, it was not fully understood by the Earthmen, who had been stuyding since they learned of it.

"We found it here," Dave announced. "You remember that cities were sighted by astronomers?"

"You found a city?" asked the English speaker. His voice was quite excited.

50

Dave suddenly realized that with their location away from a native road, the mountains to the east prevented these people from discovering a city. If they had journeyed as far south as the sunken city, they probably wouldn't have realized it was there, unless they had gone down to the beach.

"There are a number of them," he said, "all uninhabited. The technology still works, however. The machines are self-repairing. There's also plenty of grain beneath them." He referred to the hungered state of the Italians.

As if reading Dave's mind, the English-speaking fellow said, "Come with us. It's almost lunchtime."

In a communal dining hall within the main building – this was for camp operations, while others contained sleeping berths and a scientific research station including weather monitoring – lunch was served. This consisted of a thin gruel livened with native pine-like nuts, and a bread made from the native grain known to the Americans. It was not unlike corn, and baked like whole wheat.

The entire company of the Italian settlers gathered for a meal. Outer rooms like the dining hall had windows, Dave noticed, but shutters over them to keep the heat in; this was why he had observed no lights from above.

Dave Ransdell's guide, who had offered his name as Antony Tedeschi but insisted Dave call him "Teddy", due to what he mistakenly thought was an American custom, explained that they had

had to eat their livestock to get through the long winter, some 140 Earth days. Like the Americans, these were supposed to be breeding stock, and with the short summer, barely 35 Bronson Beta days, they had not been able to harvest much of the crops they'd planted, the soil being temperamental, apparently. Luckily, they'd found a few native foods they could eat, such as the grain also found in the east, and were rejoicing that spring was once again upon them.

No wonder they were malnourished, Dave Ransdell thought – no meat, their only protein being from plants in their stores, in the form of beans and legumes. The nut-like things in the gruel probably helped, as well.

The Italians were interested in what Dave knew about survival on the planet, particularly what the Americans had learned from the domed cities of the Other People. He was bombarded by questions, all of which had to be filtered through Teddy, who seemed to ignore those he didn't like, or felt were unworthy of their guest's time.

When Dave explained how the five cities in the east were connected, and what had occurred because of this – the Asiatics controlling their capital and shutting off the power to Hendron-Khorlu – the Italians were happy to hear the Asiatics had been ousted. Being Mussolini fascists, they were the natural enemy of the Eurasian coalition socialists.

Dave had to consume his meal between explanations of events back east, the gruel growing cold before he finished it.

52

After lunch, Teddy gave Dave Ransdell a tour of the habitat, which was quite efficient. It contained a small hydroponic farm, which was jury-rigged and too small to feed the two hundred or so Italians. But it was an admirable effort. This method of growing crops had been known on Earth for more than three hundred years before the end came. Nine essential ingredients had been found to be necessary for good production. The Italians seemed to know them all, for their farm was thriving.

Their weather station was similar to the one the smaller ark led by Cole Hendron had built, and their calculation of the seasons, Dave found, was pretty accurate. They knew that spring was about to arrive, and, he was told, that was the purpose of the hydroponic farm – not to feed everyone, which was an impossible task, but to get the crops started for early planting. The Italians would not be caught off guard a second summer.

The South African explorer had to admire their ingenuity. They were better prepared than the Americans had been – but seemingly at the cost of extra colonists. The League of the Last Days had chosen a thousand to make the voyage, half of which had arrived on Bronson Beta; the Italians, a mere few hundred. That left room for more equipment and supplies, even if the Italian ark was as small as the one commanded by Cole Hendron. It appeared to have been larger than *Noah's Ark*, which just under 150 feet long.

Part of their supplies was armaments, Dave saw. Unable to ignore this, he asked Teddy, "What sort of trouble did you expect to find here?"

The Italian answered, "We did not know ... with cities there might be survivors ... creatures beneath the frozen oceans ... automated defense machines."

Dave Ransdell, who knew something about war and something about Italy, found these words to be hollow. Perhaps Teddy believed them; perhaps he knew better. But whoever had armed the Italian ark had something else in mind – the conquest of a new planet. This really wasn't much of a surprise: The modern Italians, under Benito Mussolini, thought of themselves as soldiers of ancient Rome, a new Roman Empire. And their dire situation only made them more desperate.

Dave realized that he must not reveal the location of Olympus-Gorfulu, or any of the domed cities, to his hosts. Perhaps the Italians would represent no threat, once they had adequate food and shelter. But that was not his decision to make. He'd take the matter to the Central Authority, and it would be up to them to choose to contact and offer aid to the Italians, or not.

For the time being, he'd have to be a good guest, until he could get away without causing any suspicion among his hosts. He could hardly refuse their hospitality without doing so, particularly the use of a bed, since he'd been sleeping in the cramped space of the lark since leaving Olympus-Gorfulu, because it was still too cold, even during Light Night, to sleep outside without winter gear, which he lacked.

When the tour was finished, Teddy took his guest up the metal steps in the common building. They went up a number of flights, to the uppermost floor, and thence into a chamber that seemed palatial, given the size of other private rooms he had seen. There were not many of those. This was the personal quarters of a single individual, who stood near a window. The shutter was now pulled away, to allow the man there a clear view of the area below where Dave's lark sat, illuminated by floodlights powered by the atomic motor that had brought the ark to Bronson Beta.

Garbed in a military-style uniform, Dave Ransdell recognized the figure immediately. It was Benito Mussolini, Il Duce of Italy.

6

An Afternoon with Il Duce

"Welcome to Nova Italia," Benito Mussolini said to Dave Ransdell in thickly-accented English.

It should have come as no surprise to Dave that Mussolini would be aboard the Italian ark. Some of the other arks had been private projects, their passengers determined in whatever manner those doing the construction desired. Cole Hendron had personally selected his passengers; the Asiatics were of a similar phiolsophy, while the British colonists had been determined by lottery.

But Italy was a corporate state. Most of its industry was owned by the government (the fact of which the dictator was quite proud), so its ark was constructed under auspices of that government, and its passenger list created by the government. It therefore naturally included the leader of that government, Benito Mussolini.

Il Duce was a powerful presence, despite his stature, which was merely average. He appeared much as he did in newsreels Dave had seen, clothed in a uniform but now without a fez atop his shaved head. It seemed he had dressed for the occasion.

Motioning for his guest to enter with a beefy hand, he said, "Excuse me for not seeing you sooner. There were preparations to make."

At these words, an attendant came in, carrying a tray of dried fruit, cheese and wine. This was offered first to Dave, who took a few slices of each, still being hungry after the less than filling gruel, and then to Mussolini. "My apologies, Mr. Ransdell. Our selection is rather limited."

The South African explorer was surprised that there was any selection at all, considering what he had seen, and wondered if this was Mussolini's private stock. On Earth, Il Duce had created a kind of cult about himself, in which he was the chosen leader of the Italian people. Pope Pius XI had even proclaimed him "the Man of Providence"!

Therefore, Mussolini was entitled to the best of everything. His quarters reflected this, being decorated sumptuously with luxuries that the South African had seen only in the domed cities of the Other People – none of the other arks had them. Dave was sure his menu was just as selective, as well.

57

Benito Mussolini had made great strides in restoring some of Italy's lost glory to her, though he was not without his failures. The Battle for Wheat had not turned out as planned. The Battle for Land fared somewhat better. Il Duce built Italian pride by building bigger and better vehicles, such as the flying boat *Italo Balbo*, which was greeted in Chicago in 1933 with much fanfare. It was no surprise, therefore, that his ark was so well planned and constructed. But the dictator was best known for nationalizing industry, and, somewhat derisively, making the Italian trains run on time.

Mussolini gestured to a chair. "Please sit down, Mr. Ransdell."

As he did so, he said, "Dave is fine, *Signore* Mussolini."

Teddy followed suit, sitting on the opposite side of the dictator, but said nothing.

Mussolini smiled. He reminded the South African of a shark sizing up its next meal. "Benito, please. Now," he said, after seating himself, "what do you think of our little colony?"

"It's very impressive," Dave said sincerely. It put his own camp to shame, though his own ark had crashed on its side, severely hampering operations. "You've turned this into a viable settlement."

"Control of the land," said Mussolini. "That is the *fasciti* way.

"Now tell me about the progress you Americans have made. I have heard you located one of the cities seen from Earth."

Dave nodded. He chose his words carefully, recalling precisely what he had already revealed.

He did not want to be caught in a lie. "We managed to get into it – it's domed. Most of the technology is beyond our understanding. Simple things, like cars and planes, we've learned to use."

The dictator appeared quite interested in this, leaning forward in his chair. "I'd be very fascinated to hear about this. For the benefit of my people."

"I'm not an engineer," Dave replied, forcing a disappointed note into his tone. "I know how to operate the controls of my lark, but I couldn't begin to explain how it works."

"Lark? Oh, yes ... *allodola*, because the shape of your plane looks like a bird."

"Perhaps I could arrange for one of our engineers to visit you," Dave volunteered. He did not want the dictator to know that other cities existed nearby, until he had consulted with the Central Authority on the matter. After their experience with the Asiatic alliance, the explorer was now cautious of strangers.

"Or for one of ours to visit your camp," countered Mussolini.

"I'd take one with me if there was room," explained Dave evenly, "but the larks are single seaters."

"It has no weapons …."

"No. The natives seem to have possessed no weapons. Or if they did, we're unable to recognize them." Dave Ransdell saw no reason to even let the dictator know that his group had deciphered the language of the Micorites. The less he knew about the American camp, the better. Maybe he was being paranoid -- seven thousands miles separated the two camps and the Italians had no access to native technology. Still, Il Duce's reputation preceded him.

"Tell me about this city," Mussolini suggested. It was just short of being an order.

"There's not much to tell," Dave answered. "It has a dome, and it protected us from the winter weather. It's uninhabited, with no clues what happened to its original occupants."

"What did you do for food?"

"The same as your people – we found native plants we could eat. We planted Earth plants as soon as we landed, and harvested those, and, after we found the city, we moved as much of those indoors as possible. The dome acts as a greenhouse.

"And we grazed our livestock inside the dome, of course."

"Ah," breathed Mussolini, plainly envious of the Americans' landing site. "Have you encountered any others? I'm aware the French, Germans and British launched ships."

"The French ship crashed after takeoff. We watched it explode. The British ship made it; we're all living together now. They'd been captured by an Asiatic socialist alliance. We defeated it, freeing the British."

"Good, good," smiled Mussolini. Fascists and socialists were bitter enemies. There was some irony in the fact that Benito Mussolini had been a socialist until the Great War. He had been for intervention on the side of the Allied powers, unlike many of his fellow socialists, going so far as to enlist. During the war, he had been gravely wounded by an explosion, and his body still carried the shrapnel. Now, he was the very personification of socialism's Nemesis.

"We were lucky to catch them before they'd located the city themselves. The domes are impenetrable." Strictly speaking, this was true. However, the eight gates laid out in a St. George's Cross pattern were not fortified, and relatively easy to operate. Dave wanted to give Il Duce the impression that an attack on a domed city would be useless. If the Italians posed no threat, there was no harm done, but if Mussolini had plans of conquest, perhaps the impression Dave was trying to give the dictator would dissuade him.

"Society obeys Darwinian theory," Mussolini observed. "The natural law is for the strong to dominate the weak. Socialism appeals to the barbaric peoples of the east because they are weak."

Dave was slightly familiar with the dictator's philosophy. Unlike much talk of subjugation, it wasn't based on race, exactly, but culture. Some cultures were naturally superior to others, in Mussolini's view. Having seen much of the world himself, Dave couldn't disagree.

But he didn't agree with *subjugating* "lesser" cultures. What made one culture better than another, in the explorer's opinion, was how it benefited the society, not how it benefited the government and those in power. There were flaws in every type of government, some worse than others.

Seeing nothing to gain by arguing with the dictator, Dave diplomatically changed the subject.

"Before I leave, I could show your cooks or botanists plants in the area that we've found edible."

"That would be welcome," said Mussolini. "Our stores are running low. Perhaps you could arrange a sale of livestock, as well?"

"I could certainly inquire about that," Dave answered, sidestepping the obvious question of what the Italians had to offer in exchange for valuable livestock. Probably nothing except armaments, which they would likely be unwilling to give up, and which those in Olympus-Gorfulu did not find necessary. Possibly the American camp could spare a few livestock, if diplomatic relations could be established with Nova Italia – New Italy. "Do you know of any others who made it?"

Mussolini shook his head. "No one nearby. I sent scouts a hundred miles in every direction, and they found nothing." The explorer couldn't tell if Il Duce was glad not to have any neighbors, or disappointed. On Earth, the dictator had espoused the idea of *spacio vitale* – "vital space" – room for Italy to control and expand into, although it wasn't his own. Italy had claimed the entire Mediterranean region based on this principle in 1919, based on the ancient Roman Empire.

Dave did some quick calculations in his head: A hundred miles would have taken them to the mountains, which, without a road, were possibly impassable. Or perhaps they had seemed not worth the effort of attempting to cross, since no indications of habitation had been found.

The scout going south would not have reached the sunken city, either, so the Italians had no idea how close they were to a hub of five domed cities. And north – well, if Dave was right, there wouldn't be more cities for a thousand miles, if then.

Throughout the remainder of the afternoon, Mussolini interrogated Dave – that's what it seemed like, although he was very polite about it. The South African remained as vague as possible, without sounding like he was being evasive.

The dictator seemed satisfied with his answers.

Dave took the opportunity to find out more about the Italians' plans, but Il Duce was equally cagey – ambitious and proud of what he'd accomplished thus far, but unwilling to go into much detail about the future, other than stating the obvious – expansion and security. The South African did not question him too closely on either point. He neither wanted to start an unwinnable argument nor appear too curious about Il Duce's plans.

By dinnertime, Dave Ransdell had decided upon leaving as soon as possible. He intended on saying his goodbyes after the meal, and hoped that he was not invited to stay the night. This hope, it turned out, was in vain.

While eating a stew that contained some meat – Dave guessed that the Italians must have dried or frozen some of their butchered livestock to ration it out throughout the winter – Teddy told him that they hoped he would stay the night; a berth had been prepared for him.

Unable to say no, Dave accepted the invitation.

Dave Ransdell retired when the group who was entertaining him did so, and he was shown to a berth in the apartment complex building, the largest of the constructs. The Italians had used sleeping berths rather than seats in their ark, planning ahead for possible habitation. There was a communal toilet for each section, and the whole feel of the building was that of a train. The few private rooms belonged to leaders in the camp.

Dave spotted a number of empty berths as he was escorted to his own. If the ark was fully occupied upon leaving Earth, the Italians had suffered some losses. That was no surprise. His own camp had lost quite a few members themselves, most of them before they'd ever left Earth. The attack on Hendronville had cost them roughly half their number. A number of others had succumbed to various illnesses or injuries, but not many.

After a few hours in his bed, Dave consulted his wristwatch. This possessed luminous markers so it could be read in the dark. It was not an Earth timekeeper, but one of the new ones designed for the Bronson Beta day, fitted to the leather strap of Dave's old watch, which was still serviceable.

There was little point in trying to keep time by Earth standards: The day now was about fifty hours long, so a period twenty-four hours was meaningless. Hours now became one hundred twenty minutes long, giving twenty-five to a day.

64

Dave's watch read 0:80. The right half of the face was white, representing Light Day, and the left black, representing Dark Day. This was purely stylistic, as one had but to open eyes to determine if it was light or dark.

Dave waited until 1:00. On Earth, this would have been 2 AM. Then, he quietly slipped from his berth, which was an upper one, using the rung at one side to lower himself to the floor. He took ten steps, walking past the toilet, and, suddenly, a sentry at the end of the corridor came into view. When he saw the South African, he barked something in Italian. Teddy soon appeared from somewhere behind the sentry.

"No one allowed outside at night," he explained. "For your own safety." Even Teddy himself didn't believe this, judging by his tone.

Dave Ransdell was not an impatient man. But he saw no point in putting off the inevitable. He was their prisoner; he knew it, and they knew it. Being polite probably wouldn't get him anywhere. It all depended on what kind of prison he wanted to live in.

They had guessed he might leave his bed, but they couldn't have expected it: He'd given them no sign he intended to leave. He judged that he'd have no better opportunity to escape than now.

Dave threw himself at Teddy. This took the smaller man by surprise. He collapsed under Dave's might. The South African explorer launched a fist at the sentry before he could raise an alarm. It connected solidly, sending the Italian to the floor. Dave charged past the two downed men.

65

But the commotion had roused others. Once these saw what had occurred, they swarmed Dave, bringing him down despite his ferocious defense. He knocked one out cold and battered two more to the floor before he was buried under men. There were too many of them.

Finally, Dave Ransdell was knocked unconscious.

7

Trouble in Nova Italia

"You shouldn't have tried to escape," Teddy Tedeschi told Dave Ransdell through the bars of a makeshift jail cell. This had been in place before the South African explorer had arrived, but was not part of the original design of the ark, judging by the craftsmanship, which was decidedly inferior to other parts of the ship he had seen.

"If I wasn't a prisoner, I wasn't escaping," Dave retorted. "I was a guest who wanted to take a stroll."

"After midnight?" Teddy countered.

"I didn't go near anything marked 'private' or 'secure'," Dave gritted, dispensing with pleasantries. "I din't break any of your rules. You've got no reason to keep me locked up."

"Il Duce commands it. That is reason enough." After a moment, Teddy added, "No harm will come to you if you make no trouble."

"Then why are you holding me like this?" But Dave Ransdell had already guessed the answer: They were most likely studying the lark. He hoped they did not find the maps tucked beneath the seat. There was nothing else of value in it – some clothes, including a jacket, his food and water, tools, some spare parts for the motor. A pistol.

"I'll do everything in my power to make you comfortable," Teddy said. He seemed sincere enough, but it didn't matter. Mussolini called the shots, and he'd do whatever he felt necessary, and Teddy's wishes didn't amount to squat in Nova Italia. *Chance* had chosen him to speak Dave's language and no more. He was no one special, merely one of a few hundred Italians, one of the commoners.

"And how long are you planning on keeping me locked up here?" Dave asked, unable to keep the anger out of his voice.

Teddy shrugged in reply, the expression on his lean face a mixture of regret and determination.

Dave retreated to the cot, uninterested in anything the Italian had to say. The explorer doubted he even knew what was going to happen.

Dave Ransdell wasn't afraid for his life, at least not yet. If they'd wanted him dead, they would have already killed him. There were only two reasons they might kill him: He was too much trouble to keep alive, or, possibly, they had no further use for him. Dave wasn't sure that the latter was a real possibility, but it was worth keeping in mind. He was more worried about the Italians learning enough about Micorian technology to become a threat to Olympus-Gorfulu.

Hours passed. Dawn approached. Dave Ransdell would have preferred to wait until the next nightfall, almost twenty-five hours away, to attempt escape, but by then, who knew what the Italians might have discovered? He had to act fast.

Dave felt that now would not be a bad time for a break out. The night guard – there was but one – was half asleep at his station, which was also makeshift. He seemed more university dormitory Resident Advisor than prison guard, sort of a hall monitor for the floor. And he was half-asleep, like an overnight concierge at a better hotel – present if he was needed, but resting when he was not. He expected no trouble.

But he did not know Dave Ransdell.

The South African was fairly sure he would have no problem getting out of the makeshift cell. He had observed that some of the welds that held the metal bars in place were shoddy work. Of course – the cell hadn't been made to hold dangerous criminals, but more likely inebriated crewmen who needed a place to sleep it off. The bars were meant to discourage those held inside the cell, not literally prevent them from leaving. Though they might do that for most men.

Dave Ransdell was not like most men.

Dave's height topped six feet, and his shoulders were broad. His arms and legs were roped in muscles that looked like bundles of piano wires. Few words described him as well as "Herculean".

Dave put a hand on one of the iron bars and set himself. Taking a deep breath, he began to pull. Almost immediately, the bar began to give, bending slightly.

Dave pushed on it. It would never break in the middle – wresting it from its anchor point at an end was what he wanted to do. Then he could pry it back, out of the way. If he could do this to no more than three bars, he could squeeze himself through the opening. Being big had its disadvantages, too.

Finally, the weld snapped loose. Dave had to catch himself to keep himself from falling. He wasn't worried about injuring himself, but rather, waking the guard. But the fellow remained oblivious.

With a grim smile, Dave went to work on the second bar.

Fifteen minutes later, Dave Ransdell was free, or at least out of the cell. Like a cat burglar stealing along a ledge, he hoisted his massive frame through the small opening he'd created. It pinched him once, but he managed to get through without making much noise.

The sentry was blissfully unaware of what was occurring until Dave laid hands upon him. The big explorer knocked him out cold with a single punch to the jaw – the bone broke with a satisfying *crunch* – then pushed him through the opening into the cell and bent the bars back into place.

70

Moments later, Dave Ransdell stepped out into the gray haze of pre-dawn.

A single floodlight illuminated the lark. The men had worked throughout Dark Night to study it, garbed in cold weather clothing. Dave noted with grim admiration that the Italians seemed to have thought of everything.

The big South African didn't waste any time trying to reason with them. He tore into them, throwing fists. The three men went down. Two didn't get back up. Dave kicked the third in the face as he tried to rise to his feet.

Closing the cowling of the plane, the South African got into the seat and started the motor of the lark. Its sounded rough. Dave didn't like it – the workers had done something to it. What, he couldn't immediately discern. He'd have to take a closer look, and he didn't have time for that now. Revving the motor, he swung the lark around, gunned the throttle and took it into the air. Men were yelling and waving their arms below as he soared away.

Dave's elation was short lived. Almost immediately, the motor sputtered – or the equivalent of sputtered, since it was not gasoline powered – while the Italians chased the departing plane. It wasn't warm out yet – about freezing – but their blood was hot.

Dave revved the engine to keep the lark aloft. The mountains loomed in the distance. It was critical that he made it beyond them. If he had to set down on this side of them, he'd be re-captured, and, he mused, quite probably killed. He laughed mirthlessly at the thought of the fight that would take place to re-capture him.

Dave shut off the heater, anything else he could think of to give the motor more power. He nursed the lark toward the peaks ahead.

It would be a near thing.

Dave took the lark up slowly, steadily. The little red plane climbed, but not nearly as quickly as the explorer hoped.

When he saw that he lacked altitude, Dave sent the lark into a steeper climb – but not too steep, in case the motor cut out on him. He didn't want to stall the engine and flip the plane over.

Silently, he cursed the Italian mechanics who had botched things up for him.

It looked like he was going to make it. Dave gave the motor more power. The engine responded by throwing sparks into the cockpit. The plane dipped. Dave fought to keep it in the air.

It was a losing battle.

Dave kept the nose up as best he could. He watched the power drop steadily on one of the gauges.

The lark hiccupped as it flew. Sweat beaded on Dave's brow despite the cold of the cockpit. It took all of his skill to get the little plane to limp over the divide. Finally, he did it. Then he began looking for a place to set down.

The explorer reduced power to the motor, and, keeping the nose up, started to descend. He was practically gliding, feeding the motor just enough power to keep it from stalling.

72

Smoke was beginning to fill the cockpit, and Dave had to crack the transparent metal bubble to vent it. Cold air rushed in and slapped him in the face. This had an invigorating effect on the big man. He hadn't slept much since arriving in Nova Italia, and was tired, even if it didn't show in his actions.

Beyond the mountains was a valley. Dave pointed the lark in that direction. He brought the plane down safely – not his best landing but under the circumstances, quite an acceptable one. He let the little ship roll to a stop, shut off the engine.

Disembarking the cockpit, he pulled the cowling away from the motor and gave it a look. It didn't appear too bad. Nothing important seemed to be missing – probably much couldn't be, or he'd never have gotten the lark in the air in the first place. But Dave realized it was going to take some work to get the plane running again, if ever.

There was no hurry, having left his pursuers far behind. According to Mussolini, his people hadn't crossed the mountains. That meant Dave was safe.

Airing out the cockpit, he climbed into it, started up the heater again and went to sleep. He needed a clear head to fix the motor – he was something of a mechanic – and it was just too cold to get any work done now.

It was still light out when Dave Ransdell awoke. He checked his watch. About three hours – three Bronson Beta hours – had passed since he'd landed. He was still tired but more rest could wait. His stamina was nearly superhuman and he felt alert enough now to tackle the problem of the motor. The temperature had climbed a good ten degrees, and he began looking for signs of trouble.

Dave was no expert in Micorian technology – he knew as much as anyone else who wasn't a physicist or a mechanic, more than most; but was by no means an expert. Certainly, he knew more about gas-powered motors than this type.

Dave started by looking for obvious trouble, and found components that showed signs of heat damage – blackened areas. These would have to be replaced; he had nothing with which he could repair such modules, even if he thoroughly understood what was wrong with them.

This was not as bad as it seemed. He carried a number of spare parts for just such an emergency, in a compartment behind the seat. These were as easy to replace as spark plugs in an Earth gasoline motor, and Dave hoped he was carrying the right replacements.

He then went over the power transfer components with a fine-toothed comb, because at least part of the problem lay there, even if it didn't look like it. The explorer found some damage that he might have otherwise overlooked.

Removing one module at a time, Dave looked through the spare parts for a match. He found one, replaced the damaged component and moved onto the next. There was also a small tool set stashed with the replacement parts, which facilitated the work.

The third time out, Dave wasn't so lucky. Nothing in the spare parts compartment matched what he needed. With no other recourse, the South

74

African removed the dash in the cockpit and began hunting parts. He could do without most of the instrumentation, and the heater, if he had to. The Italians seemed to have searched his spare clothing but left it in place. His fur-lined pilot's jacket, which he'd worn in the Great War, was there. He had put it on, out of habit, when he'd gone to sleep. He was glad he did, since he was working outdoors now.

Dave spent the better part of the day cannibalizing the instrument panel to repair the motor. He was just about finished when he heard noise. This startled him, as there should be nothing creating sounds nearby. Bronson Beta was a dead world but for the animal life that came from Earth.

Climbing atop the crimson lark's fuselage for a better view, Dave scanned the area with his clear blue eyes. The noise, he found, was coming from the west. He watched as figures wended their way through the vegetation that was just beginning to awaken from its winter slumber.

It was the Italians! The goddamned Italians had followed him over the mountains! They must have found a pass – they must have not used it before because they'd had no reason to do so.

They weren't far away now – less than a mile, probably closer to half a mile.

Dave hurriedly put the last module in place and secured it. He did this carefully, despite his haste. If he messed this up, he would fall into the Italians' hands again.

Replacing the cowling, he climbed into the cockpit and started the motor. It wasn't perfect but it sounded better than it had before. Pointing the nose east, Dave gunned the motor and got the lark into the air once more.

It ran smooth for about a minute, then it started grumbling. It still sounded better than before, but not as good as it should have. Dave had no confidence that he could keep the ship in the air for any length of time. But even an hour would put him out of the reach of the Italians – even if he took it slow and easy, he'd make a couple of hundred miles. And once he was out of sight, he could turn the lark another direction and his pursuers would never locate him in case he had to land again. He expected to. He'd have liked to given the motor the once-over before take off, but that wasn't meant to be.

As he flew, the South African pondered how the Italians had reached him so soon. They'd covered the hundred miles or so in six Earth hours. Then it struck him: They must have motored vehicles they'd brought from Earth, and driven these to the foothills.

Ruefully, he had to admit he'd underestimated them. Well, he'd have the last laugh.

Dave flew for ten minutes, keeping his speed at a little over one hundred miles per hour. He'd gotten it up to two hundred, initially, but didn't like the way the motor struggled. As he banked to turn south, in the direction of Olympus-Gorfulu, he spied something out of the corner of an eye – a dome! One of the domed cities.

Reaching beneath the seat, his hand sought his map. It was gone! The Italians had found it, confiscated it. That made Dave's mission even more urgent. With his map, Mussolini would know where Olympus-Gorfulu and the other cities were located.

An idea came to Dave, and he brought the lark sharply around to point it at the dome in the distance. The steady drone of the motor stuttered. Unpleasant noises came from the engine compartment, but there was no sparks or smoke yet. The little plane began to descend and Dave couldn't stop it.

8

The Necropolis

Dave Ransdell came to consciousness slowly. His robin's-egg blue eyes fluttered, then fully opened. What had happened? He couldn't recall.

A valley filled with tall yellow grass that was now fallen over, in hibernation for the winter months, greeted his sight. Now he remembered: His lark had crashed. One of his jury-rigged parts must have given out; the plane had lost power too suddenly for him to bring it down safely. Or maybe he'd missed one of the connections the Italians mechanics had fooled with.

Dave put a hand to his throbbing head; it came away bloody. Crimson fluid stained his fingers.

There wasn't much blood. Not enough to worry him. He'd been shot down twice during the

Great War, and injured both times. This didn't seem too bad.

Now Dave realized what had awoken him. It was the wild whoops of his Italian pursuers. They were nearly upon him. Hauling his mighty frame from the cockpit, he vaulted to the ground. He stumbled, fell, a little dizzy. Forcing himself to his feet, the explorer cast his gaze about until he spotted the dome of the City of the Other People, and, after grabbing his canteen, ran for it.

Ten minutes later, Dave Ransdell was at the dome. He had covered the mile in good time, he thought. Considering his head hurt and his balance felt off, at any rate. He had spied one of the city's eight gates as he ran for it, and went there. This worked in much the same manner as those in the east, and he had no trouble getting in. The fastener was a complicated-looking affair that was easy to use, once one knew how, rather like a puzzle once solved. This would buy him enough time to do what he needed to do.

Inside the dome, Dave slumped down against the wall of the gatehouse, and gulped in deep breaths of air once he had fastened the gate once more. The run had winded him more than it should have. He was light headed. But, the trickle of blood from his head wound had stopped. Perhaps he had a mild concussion. Or maybe he just needed rest.

As Dave sat and caught his breath, the Italians arrived. First, they beat on the gate, while yelling at the South African – undoubtedly to let them in –

and those that could not reach the gate beat upon the transparent metal of the dome. There were dozens of them, the explorer saw. Mussolini had recognized the value of Micorian technology, as Dave feared he would. And he'd led the Italians straight to it.

Dave could not help but smile a grim smile at the futile efforts of the men. When they drew pistols, and shot at the dome, their bullets bouncing off it without even leaving a mark, his smile became a chuckle. The transparent metal of the dome was practically indestructible. The only thing believed to be able to damage it – and this hadn't been tested – was the heat of an atomic motor, the kind that had propelled the arks to Bronson Beta.

Once he had rested sufficiently, Dave drew himself up to his feet, and, ignoring the shouting Italians, began to make his way along the wide avenue into the city proper.

The City of the Other People was incredibly quiet. The dome wasn't precisely soundproof, but it cut down on noise from the outside considerably, like a closed window in a house. The shouting of the Italians faded after Dave had gone a hundred yards. He hadn't bothered looking back to see if they had stopped shouting; it didn't matter. They were now irrelevant, and, if things went the way Dave expected them to, he would soon be beyond their reach permanently.

He didn't expect the gate to stymie them forever, however. Tony Drake and Eliot James had figured out how to open them, and the Italians would, eventually. Dave probably didn't need to hurry – he was jogging along the wide empty streets – but he didn't lollygag either.

The explorer passed the power station that indicated that this was the capital of the five cities, as Olympus-Gorfulu was back east. Each of the satellite cities merely had distributing, or relay, stations. He made a mental note of this fact and continued on his way.

Then, a sound reached the explorer's ears. Involuntarily, he started. Had the Italians found their way in so soon? He thought he'd have at least half an hour to himself.

But no, no further noise came. If it were the Italians, then certainly there would have been more noise, as they ran through the city looking for him.

If it was not the Italians ....

Dave Ransdell paused, considered his options. Surely, a few minutes would make no difference, and he cautiously proceeded in the direction of the solitary sound, his ears pricked up for further noise but none came. He walked for a hundred yards; certainly the noise had originated no further, he felt.

Gazing about, he saw the entrance to the underground granary.

There was no sign of movement there, no sounds emanating from within it. Yet ... the door was open. Had the door to the vault beneath Hendron-Khorlu or Olympus-Gorfulu been open? He couldn't recall, but he didn't think so. Did that mean this door being open held any special significance?

Maybe, maybe not. "Human" error might be responsible. The human settlers had yet to determine what had become of the Micorites, how they had spent their final days. It was not beyond possibility that a door had been left open accidentally.

Still, the doorway beckoned him.

After a moment of thinking, Dave answered its summons and walked toward it. He wished he had his pistol – an M1911 Browning Automatic he'd acquired during the war – but the Italians had confiscated it. He'd brought it along out of habit, despite not expecting to find anything alive in his journey of exploration.

The South African's best guess, as he proceeded toward the open doorway, was that he would find one of the Micorian machines doing something. Some were fully automated and most were self-repairing. None had thus far proven dangerous.

Dave was also fairly sure none of the Italians had beaten him here – unless some had gone around to another gate. Each city possessed eight of them, laid out like St. George's Cross, so it was not impossible that an exceptionally smart or exceptionally lucky Italian had cracked the fastener on a nearby gate and beat Dave here. But the South African explorer didn't think so. He had traveled in more or less a straight line, and they'd have had to traverse the curvature of the dome, which was about five miles in diameter.

Finding nothing inside the doorway, Dave proceeded to the elevator, ignoring the steps. There were lots of these. The temperature, fairly pleasant inside the dome above, steadily rose as the elevator descended. The cage went down for a long time, until finally, Dave found himself in a granary like the one beneath Hendron-Khorlu, which had been discovered by Higgins, a botanist. A similar vault had been found under Olympus-Gorfulu, but this was kept in reserve, while the granary of Hendron-Khorlu was drawn upon throughout the winter; it had become the farm of the human settlers, in every sense of the word. The colonists had used but a fraction of the food stored there. Certainly the supply of but one of the five cities would last for the lifetime of every settler, and probably every child of every settler.

As Dave turned to leave, something caught his attention: a door where there should be no door. He had been in the granary beneath Hendron-Khorlu, there was no door in the vault where this one was. Was there a matching door in the storage vault beneath Olympus-Gorfulu? He had never been down there, and no one had mentioned such a door. No complete survey of the facility beneath Olympus-Gorfulu had been made because it appeared to be identical to that of Hendron-Khorlu. But this one was tucked away in a corner, and if he had not been searching the granary he might not have seen it.

Intrigued, Dave investigated. After a few moments, he got the door open, and what he saw left him speechless: rows and rows of tubes, each one containing a perfectly preserved Micorite!

There were thousands – tens of thousands, perhaps hundreds of thousands – of them! He had found the crypt of the natives of Bronson Beta!

9

Desperate Escape

It had long been a mystery, what had happened to the last of the corpses of the Micorites as the rogue star Borak approached their planetary system. Even if the race had undertaken some sort of mass suicide, which was the leading theory among the Earthmen, a few would have to remain behind to dispose of the bodies, since none had been found in any of the five cities in the east. The hermetically sealed environments, combined with the intense cold of the voyage through open space, should have protected these expected corpses. No satisfactory explanation had been found for the absence of bodies, and eventually, the matter had been forgotten.

But now Dave had found the answer: They had crawled into personal crypts and killed themselves – by gas, probably. One of their gasses, *klul*, produced a euphoric feeling. Probably this had been mixed with something toxic, the explorer guessed.

A noise – far away, but inside the massive crypt. Dave didn't like the sound of it. It could have been something being dropped, but more likely, a machine engaging. It reminded him of a furnace coming on. He wondered if his presence had somehow triggered an automatic machine – what would it do?

Deciding he had tarried too long underground, he began back toward the surface. He checked his watch – and silently cursed himself for the time he had wasted. Unless they were completely incompetent, the Italians would almost certainly be inside the dome by now.

Well, they had to check every building for Dave, while he knew exactly where he was going.

When he reached the surface, Dave Ransdell heard the Italian men searching nearby, but they were not in sight. Now, he did not take the time to curse himself for wasting so much time below the city. Instead, he went into action: He headed in the opposite direction, and, when he came to the end of the block, turned toward the city's aerodrome. Every city had the same basic layout – at least those in the east had – and this one seemed to, as well, based on what he'd seen thus far.

Dave peeked down along the next avenue. No one was in sight. He hurried across the street.

Before he'd reached the other side, a voice shouted, "*Eccolo!*"

It wasn't hard to guess what it meant – he'd been spotted.

As he began to run, Dave glanced down the street: One of the Italians was pointing at him with a pistol. The air cracked with the launch of a bullet, which spanged on the hard street somewhere behind Dave. A second bullet followed, but he was out of sight by then, and sprinting away from his pursuers.

It didn't take the Italians long to organize and chase after the big South African explorer. Half a dozen of them were close behind Dave as he ran, firing their Beretta M1934 semi-automatic pistols. These were literally the most modern firearm available, having been produced the year the Earth was destroyed, firing 9 mm Corto ammunition. They were very popular in Europe as the end neared.

Dave ran for the aerodrome, ignoring inviting byways where he might lose his pursuers. The South African didn't worry about being clever now. If he pulled some trick that didn't work as he planned, the Italians would have him. They might want him alive, to explain the Micorian technology to them, but the Italians were a hot-blooded people, and Dave wouldn't be surprised if he were shot in the heat of the moment. It seemed likely one might shoot to wound and instead kill him by accident. It was nothing to gamble on, anyway.

Dave Ransdell ran as fast as he was able – he could rest once he got inside a lark. There was every reason to believe that this city, constructed in the same plan as those located in the east, would have its own aerodrome, and that aerodrome would be filled with planes. All the big explorer had to do was get there, commandeer a lark, and fly away. He was certain the Italians hadn't yet cracked the controls of Micorian craft. They might, within hours, but Dave was confident they wouldn't pursue him – the larks weren't armed and their Il Duce Mussolini would want to see the captured ships as soon as possible. And that was assuming there were any pilots present. Dave figured there were. It was safer that way.

After his errand for Sven Bronson, delivering proof of impending doom to Cole Hendron, Dave Ransdell had been in many dangerous situations, on every continent on Earth – with the exception of Antarctica. He'd made a habit of overestimating his opponents rather than underestimating them, if he was forced to choose between the two. He was a good judge of the ways things were, including sizing up an enemy, but there were simply some things that could not be known, and had to be estimated. The big man erred on the side of caution whenever possible.

Although he made no fancy maneuvers to lose his pursuers, Dave turned at every corner he could, without going out of his way. If he continued going in a straight line as far as he was able, the Italians would have clear shots at him – and take them. So some evasive actions were necessary.

Occasionally, a bullet struck somewhere behind him. One passed overhead. Dave was just keeping out of range of the Berettas. The South

African explorer pushed his mighty frame for all he could, and stayed one step ahead of the pot shooting of the Italians. He might have hoped they'd run out of ammo before they caught him, but there were too many of them for this to occur, and too few shots. They knew they had the advantage and were enjoying using it.

Dave's legs ached, his lungs burned but he kept moving. More than just his own life was at stake: The Italians could launch a sneak attack on Olympus-Gorfulu with what they obtained from this city. He had to make it back there to warn everyone. Perhaps war could be forestalled with diplomacy. It would be a shame to doom Bronson Beta to the same problems that had plagued Earth – a tragedy.

The big South African rounded a corner – and found a group of Italians there!

The four men were only a few yards away, and stationary. They appeared as startled as Dave when he appeared from around the corner. He didn't stop, didn't even slow. He barreled into them. They were close enough together that, by reaching out his arms wide, he was able to bowl all of them over at once. In such a pose, Dave went down with them, carried by the force of his own momentum.

The one in front, the one whom the explorer collided with lay on the street, mumbling incoherently, was stunned. The other three were relatively unharmed, and quickly returned to their feet. When they did, they found Dave Ransdell waiting for them.

Not exactly waiting: The South African grasped hold of the nearest arm and propelled its owner in the direction of the other two men. He clipped one, while the other stepped aside. That one fumbled to retrieve his Beretta, which he'd dropped on the street.

He had his hand upon it when Dave brought his booted foot down on the Italian's face. He collapsed without a sound.

The big man whirled, found the remaining two men moving warily toward him. They didn't make the same mistake their comrade had – diverting their attention from their enemy to retrieve their fallen weapons. They separated as they approached the South African, so that he couldn't take them both out with a single attack.

"Come on," Dave Ransdell gritted. "Let's get this over with." There was no fear in his voice, only impatience. The last time two men gave him much trouble, he'd still been a teenager.

Both men rushed him at once. Dave threw his fist at one man and raised his arm to ward off a blow from the other. His strike landed like a thunderbolt. The Italian's jaw broke, and the fellow staggered about, confused by the pain.

Dave turned his attention to the second man. He caught the incoming fist in one of his massive hands, and began to squeeze. The Italian crumbled. His knees sagged and he began to drop to the street. His free hand flailed at Dave, to no avail.

"Smile for the camera," the big South African said. Although he did not comprehend the words, the Italian looked up at Dave when he spoke. A big fist came down and struck him squarely in the face, breaking his nose and knocking him out.

Going to the fellow with the broken jaw – he had stopped staggering about and was now leaning the wall of a building for support – Dave threw a fist into a kidney.

With a howl, the Italian collapsed onto the metallic street, and writhed there, a combination of gasps and curse words escaping his lips.

Seeing the one whom he'd kicked just coming to, Dave went to him and gave him another kick in the head. He promptly collapsed once again.

Picking up a fallen Beretta, Dave saw that Roman numerals had been stamped onto it: XIII. He recalled that Italy had re-started its calendar in 1922, when Benito Mussolini became Prime Minister.

He hefted the weapon in his hand. It weighed about a pound and a half. Dave Ransdell knew that the M1934 was a good gun, if properly cared for. It had been expressly designed for the Italian Army, *Esercito Italiano*, by the Beretta Company in order to not lose a valuable customer when the Italians were impressed by the German Walther PP pistol. So Armi Beretta SpA, which had a four hundred year history but had only begun producing pistols during the Great War, designed the M1934 as a rival sidearm. The Italian Army was pleased with this, and accepted it as their official weapon as the Bronson planets neared Earth for the second time.

Pocketing two pistols and carrying the other two, Dave Ransdell resumed his desperate escape.

He had lost valuable time fighting the four Italians. The others who were chasing him had caught up to him. He was pinned down in a doorway not far from the aerodrome. He kept them at bay with the pistols he had confiscated, but he was badly outnumbered.

Despite being well hidden, a lucky bullet could strike him at any moment. Already, shrapnel from the edge of the doorway had pelted his arm. Twice. This didn't do much damage but it was painful. The wounds had leaked enough blood to stain his shirt and leather flying jacket, but little more.

Dave opened the door behind him, and went inside the building. Quickly fastening the latch, he hurried through the lobby, disappearing before the Italians, who suspected an ambush, arrived at the entrance. He exited the rear of the building before his pursuers had figured out how to unlatch the door, and began running for the aerodrome, which was now in sight from his new position. It was still a good run to it, but his destination was in sight. This knowledge fueled his exhausted body.

If this airfield were anything like the ones Dave knew, it would be filled with planes. Opening the big door of one of the hangars, he found a lark, virtually identical to the one he'd flown west. This one was canary yellow, with black trim, in contrast to the crimson one he'd claimed as his own in Olympus-Gorfulu.

He climbed into the cockpit, thumbed the ignition. He had to do this a few times to get the old motor started. Luckily, the lark had been double sheltered, inside the dome and then inside the hangar. Nothing had gotten inside the cowling to discourage it from starting. A gasoline engine would have been impossible to start without priming it. This was not a gasoline motor.

Finally, the motor started up, hummed like a happy bee. Dave put the plane in motion and pointed it at the hangar doorway.

Dave got the lark outside and onto the Micorian equivalent of tarmac when Italians began pouring onto the field. They pelted the little ship with bullets as it taxied about but its metal hide was impervious to such impacts, and Dave ignored these as he gunned the motor. The lark lifted gracefully into the air. Dave looped it around and pointed it east.

His last thought before the domed city was lost to his sight was that he wished he'd had time to disable all the other planes there.

10

Re-Birth

It was exactly one Bronson Beta Year after the emergence of humans onto their new planet when a breakthrough in the Sleeping Sickness was made. A number of doctors had been working for the past two days on the problem, which had now killed four. Hargreaves, one of the British doctors, rushed into Dodson's office, papers in hand. "I think we have the answer, Charles!" the Englishman exclaimed.

"Yes, yes," rumbled Dodson, who tugged at the salt-and-pepper hair on his prodigious jowls in anticipation.

"It's a pollen allergy!"

Dodson paused pulling at the wiry hair of his pork chop sideburns for a moment, in astonishment, then resumed the nervous action. Of course! This was why the Sleeping Sickness had struck but once in the entire year! It was a seasonal allergy tied to the beginning of spring! How simple – yet how elusive. With no more cases, it had soon been forgotten by the Americans, as the threat of the Asiatic alliance loomed and the two camps found one another and united, relocating to the city that would become known as Hendron-Khorlu. Some had considered it an early attack by the Asiatics, but it truly did not fit the pattern of their latter assault on the American camp with gas.

"You know that some of the plant life here is toxic to humans," said Hargreaves – the wiry botanist Higgins had established that – "it is these same plants whose pollen is causing the Sleeping Sickness. Every one of our recent cases had been outside prior to suffering from the illness. That was the clue that provided the answer."

"Good work, Hargreaves," Dodson thundered. "Now you should be able to find a cure."

The Englishman nodded his head. "We're already working on it. A blocker similar to piperoxan should stop these attacks." Piperoxan was an H1 antihistamine, which had been discovered shortly before the destruction of the Earth. This type of drug blocked the histamine action at the H1 receptor, alleviating allergic symptoms. "We just need to find the right chemicals. We tried piperoxan, but it had no effect. These native pollens must work somewhat differently than we expected."

"Really good work, Hargreaves," Dodson reiterated. "The pall hanging over Re-Birth will be a little less thick because of your work. I'll go inform Tony Drake."

Outside the hospital, the Re-Birth celebration was in full swing. Most of the nearly twelve hundred inhabitants of Olympus-Gorfulu were in the city square, where a picnic was in progress – it was noon of a Light Day – and Micorian music played.

In each of the four satellite cities, a bust of Lagon Itol, the architect of the plan to save the Micorites, stood at one of the city gates – the gate that faced Olympus-Gorfulu, the hub or capital of the five domed cities. In Olympus-Gorfulu, the bust occupied a prominent place in the square in the center of the city, and it was around this statue that everyone gathered. For although he had failed to save his own race, Lagon Itol had inadvertently saved the human race, for without his domed cities, the Earth refugees would have perished over the long, cold winter of Bronson Beta. He was celebrated as a national hero as much as Cole Hendron, the man who had designed the arks that had brought the Americans to Bronson Beta.

Peter Vanderbilt, standing arm in arm with Marian Jackson, the brave young woman who had instigated the revolt in Midian, watched as Tony Drake stepped up on a chair in the square to address the crowd. The redheaded woman had initially set her sights on Tony, determined to marry him, becoming his second wife, for the ratio of men to women was such that if every woman wanted a husband, some would have to share with other women. After some months of pursuit, Marian finally accepted that Tony was a one-woman man, and soon latched onto Peter, who was similar in the fundamentals to Tony: They both hailed from New York and both had money – on Earth, that is. Here on Bronson Beta, they both had a measure of responsibility and power. Both men were brave and emotionally strong. So Peter seemed like a natural choice for Marian after Tony did not respond to her advances, despite the fact that he was twenty years older than she. No one was surprised by their union.

On Marian's shoulder sat Clara the monkey. She had latched onto Marian, perhaps sensing her as a kindred spirit: Both were stowaways on the *Mayflower II*.

"What's he going to say, dear?" Marian asked her husband as Clara tugged at her finger.

"I don't know," answered Peter. "I didn't know he was going to say anything. He has some closing remarks he's going to give this evening, but this ... I have no idea."

"Pardon me for interrupting the celebration," Tony Drake shouted, in order to be heard over the residual noise as those gathered quieted down. "I'm sure you all heard enough from me this morning, when I kicked off Re-Birth. But I just received some news that I know all of you will want to hear:

"The cause of the Sleeping Sickness has been found! It's a pollen allergy, and now that Dr. Dodson and his team have discovered this, it's only a matter of time before a cure and preventative will be found."

The crowd roared their approval.

"Now I'll let you return to the festivities," Tony shouted over the tumult, and stepped down from his impromptu platform.

"Another reason for celebration," Eliot James murmured to himself with obvious glee on his aquiline features.

Pierre Duquesne, who happened to be standing nearby, overheard the comment and remarked, "Indeed. Wonderful news." Marlene Dietrich was absent, preparing her theater group for a performance that evening., and the Frenchman had other female companionship now.

Shirley Cotton, beside the French physicist, breathed, "Thank God." The young Negro woman could often be found in his company. His intellect fascinated her, and though he considered himself too old for romance with her – despite Marlene's permission to take on a second wife – Duquesne was flattered by the attention. Their relationship was a practical one, as well as being a stimulating one, and merely platonic.

The old Frenchman knew that whomever Shirley eventually chose, they would have to contend with Dodson. After she had saved old Dodson's life when Hendronville in Michigan was attacked, the two had remained close, developing a close bond that would never be broken. More than mere friendship, their relationship was more like that of father and daughter.

Rejoining his wife, Tony Drake saw young Jack Taylor wending his way through the crowd. Jack was Tony's aide-de-camp, having been taken under the older man's wing on Earth. His normally pleasant face wore a determined look now. The leader of Olympus-Gorfulu expected news of trouble to come out of the young redhead's mouth. He was surprised when Jack announced, "Dave Ransdell just radioed in. He'll be landing in a few minutes."

Tony Drake, Eve Hendron, Peter Vanderbilt and Jack Taylor gathered at Olympus-Gorfulu's aerodrome to meet Dave Ransdell's plane. Seeing the yellow-and-black coloring of the descending lark, Eve asked, "That's not the plane he took off in, is it? I thought he'd taken a red one."

Her husband nodded. "Are you sure that's Dave?" Tony asked Peter. Air traffic control had been placed under the purview of the Safety office.

"I'm sure," the New Yorker affirmed. "Even if I didn't recognize his voice, I'd know it was him – he knows things only one of us Argonauts would know. "

The group watched as the colorful plane rolled to a stop, then hurried out to meet it. Tony lagged behind, keeping pace with his wife who was burdened with a growing child in her belly. Her swell was quite noticeable by now. By the time the couple reached the lark, the big South African was already out of the ship, and stood on the ground, accepting welcoming slaps on the back from Peter and Jack.

"I'm glad you're here," Dave said to Tony, then he glanced at Peter. "You, too."

His gaze did not fall upon Eve, and the young woman understood why. She accepted that there might always be a gulf between her and Dave, after she'd chosen Tony over him.

"Other humans made it here," the big explorer announced. "Italians." He then recounted his adventures out west, momentarily forgetting to mention the Ransdellosaurus he'd discovered by accident. His voice took on a rueful tone when he described the Italians finding the domed city because of him – Fecnar, if he'd read the signs therein correctly. He was not as well versed in Micorese as some.

"Well, you didn't have a choice," Tony said immediately, with sincerity. He had nothing but respect for the South African, always had, and always would. "The important thing is that you're all right ... and you were able to warn us. I'll call a meeting of the Central Authority, and we'll figure out how to handle this."

"There's something else," Dave said, putting a hand on Tony's arm that felt like a steel vise. "Fecnar was a capital like Olympus-Gorfulu is. Beneath it –"

A voice shouting from across the field interrupted the South African explorer. Everyone turned to see Higgins there. The botanist was a scrawny little fellow but he possessed the endurance and tenacity of a mountain goat, along with its interest in climbing. He was barely breathing hard despite having run across the entire airfield, and, they later learned, from the central section of the city.

"Tony, you've got to come," Higgins said. His face was furled with worry.

"What is it?" The leader of Olympus-Gorfulu's first thought was that the Italians had arrived – but it was much too soon for that, according to Dave Ransdell's account.

"It's the Other People," exclaimed Higgins. "They've returned!"

11

The People a Million Years Dead

Without explaining, Edgar Higgins turned and began back toward the city square. His pace bespoke of urgency, and the others quickly followed.

"What are you talking about?" Tony Drake demanded, hurrying to catch up the wiry fellow.

"I was inspecting the granary," the scrawny botanist explained without breaking his stride, "as I do every month. I heard a noise. I investigated and came to a door in one corner of the chamber. I'd never seen it before. No one had ever surveyed the entire granary, since it was very similar to the one I'd discovered under Hendron-Khorlu.

"Everyone – myself included – assumed them to be identical since they appeared identical upon a casual inspection. But they are not, not exactly.

"During my routine checks, I kept to the same spots and therefore never saw this door before. For some reason, I took a different path and found this previously unknown door.

"Opening this, I found a crypt that contained thousands of glass cylinders, each holding a Micorite.

"And then I saw – one of them!"

"What do you mean?" asked Peter Vanderbilt.

"One of them was awake!" exclaimed Higgins. "Don't you see – they didn't die; they only went to sleep! That's why the granaries were built – to feed the Micorites when they awoke!"

Dave Ransdell realized that it had been a Micorite he had heard in the vault beneath Fecnar, not a machine, not an Italian. The sleeping Other People were awakening from their million-year sleep!

Professor Philbin, the linguist, was waiting for Tony and selected members of the Central Authority at the entrance to the massive underground vault. This included Dodson, who was in charge of social policies, and Duquesne, who, though not a member of the Central Authority, would never forgive Tony for not including him, so the leader of the Earthmen had him summoned, as well.

Also present was Kyto, Tony Drake's former manservant, who saw to the city's operations (aided by Ben King, who had been the ark's purser, and now oversaw logistics and administrative support). Not even Tony himself had suspected that the Japanese man had been sent to the U.S. as a spy, and performed that duty, until he had embraced the American way of life.

Kyto was actually quite competent in a number of areas, and he was the natural choice to succeed his former employer when Tony replaced Cole Hendron as leader after that illustrious personage's death. For example, Kyto, possessing a black belt in *karate*, was almost certainly the most skilled hand-to-hand combatant in the city, though he may have had a few rivals among the Japanese who had belonged to the Asiatic alliance.

The eight men – Peter Vanderbilt, head of the Safety Office, was the final man – entered the vault and boarded the elevator. This worked by a means unknown to the Earthmen, possessing no cables. One theory that had been advanced was that the cage was suspended by means of static electricity or magnetism, or even a combination of the two. The Micorites were much more advanced in physics than humans, using a motive force unknown on Earth, and not fully understood by the Earth colonists.

The elevator began to descend. It was a long way down. There were also stairs, but the elevator must have been constructed for freight – it would have been backbreaking work to carry the tons and tons of grain down those steps to the granary below.

As the cage dropped, Dave Ransdell revealed what he had been interrupted in saying: "I found the same thing in the city in the west. I was about to tell you that there might be a similar crypt beneath Olympus-Gorfulu, since, it, too, is a capital of five cities. But I had no idea the Micorites were merely sleeping.

"My guess is that only the capitals have the crypts – or, I should say, slumber chambers. That's why we never found such a room beneath Hendron-Khorlu. Only the capitals have them."

"I'd say your theory has been confirmed," vouchsafed Tony Drake in a sober tone.

"We should have known something was amiss," Duquesne put in.

"What do you mean?" asked Dave.

"Two hundred million people," the Frenchman said, quoting the population of Micor at the time Borak arrived, according to the final census, "could never have lived in just these five cities. There had to be more. You could fit no more than ten million persons in each city, I would estimate. There must even be more cities than the five Mr. Ransdell found in the west."

Silence held reign for some moments as the eight men pondered this. The continent was a large one. There was plenty of room for other arrangements of five cities, not to mention the other three landmasses of Bronson Beta, Polus, Borealis and Australis.

Finally, Tony Drake spoke.

"You say you only saw one of them?" he asked Higgins, anxious to know what they would face when they reached the granary room.

The scrawny botanist nodded. "Only one, for certain. But I had the impression there were more, farther back in the chamber."

"I wonder how they will feel about squatters?" asked Peter Vanderbilt.

This was the very same thought the other seven men pondered.

It was quite hot in the bowels of the underground complex beneath Olympus-Gorfulu, more than one hundred degrees Fahrenheit. At its deepest point, it was two miles below the surface and the elevator covered this distance rather rapidly, in about six minutes. The men perspired even before reaching the lowest level. Most of this was due to the heat.

It was safe to say that apprehension filled the cage. Only the most foolhardy of men would not feel anxious about meeting alien beings for the first time. Add to that the fact that the Earthmen had invaded the home of the Micorites – unknowingly, of course – and the atmosphere in the elevator was an uneasy one.

Balancing these feelings was the belief that the Micorites were of an enlightened nature, based on what had been translated of their writings. Professor Philbin, who had spearheaded the project, creating a small library of translated works, said, "I think we should be optimistic about this." There was a nervous quality to his tone. "We have no reason to believe they are a violent people."

Dave Ransdell had to give the university professor credit: He had volunteered for this mission, despite being nervous and it being outside his normal duties. Tony Drake put this thought into words: "I appreciate you offering to do the translating, Professor."

"Interpreting," corrected Philbin. "Translating pertains to documents."

Ignoring the unnecessary – in his mind – correction, Tony continued. "As the man who has done the most work with the Micorian language, you have the best chance of making our intentions clear."

"And theirs," added Philbin nervously.

"And theirs," repeated Tony, keeping the growing exasperation he felt out of his voice.

The elevator came to an abrupt stop. Tony Drake led the way out, followed by Peter Vanderbilt, naturally because he was in charge of security, and by Dave Ransdell, naturally because he was the sort of man who faced danger head on.

"This shall be most interesting," pronounced Duquesne, stepping from the cage in his peculiar waddle seemingly caused by his barrel chest. With his long arms dangling, he was almost a comic sight.

The remaining four men were close behind this leading triumvirate, which parted to allow Higgins forward, to show them where the door to the sleeping chamber was located.

The hum of mighty machines laboring came to their ears before they had reached the desired spot. Light spilled forth from the cracked door. Higgins stepped aside to allow Tony Drake to peer in, but

Dave Ransdell moved closer first. Tony joined him, gently nudging the giant aside, and Dave let him; he had momentarily forgotten his place. Tony had every right to have first look at the goings-on within the so-called crypt.

There were now dozens – perhaps hundreds – of Micorites awake! They milled about, stretching stiff limbs, and speaking to one another. These specimens resembled those found in their art to a large degree: Their skin was brown and pinkish, like Caucasians, but their facial features resembled no race of Earth. Their fingers were arranged slightly differently, the thumb being on the outside, rather than the inside.

Tony, who knew some of their lingo, made out snatches of their conversation over the hum of the machines – they were glad to be awake again, and that their planet had reached a stable orbit.

With a hand and a backward glance over his shoulder, Tony Drake gestured Philbin to come forward. The two entered together, pushing the door open wide. Dave, having been at Tony's side, came next, followed by Peter Vanderbilt and the others.

A murmur ran through the drowsy Micorites upon seeing the humans. A few retreated. One raised his voice and shouted to be heard over the machinery, which seemed to be responsible for awakening the slumbering people. "Do not be alarmed! These beings have settled on our world after their own was destroyed, in much the same way Borak disrupted our solar system. They are a primitive people. There are only a thousand of them."

Professor Philbin yelled to the Other People, "We mean you no harm. We did not know any of your race still lived when we came here."

Another murmur, this one filled with surprise that an alien to their world spoke their language. Philbin explained, "We used your children's teaching units to learn your language. Most of us speak it, to varying degrees."

One of the Micorites stepped forward. Unlike many of the others, he was clothed. His garb was a simple gown-like affair. Tony guessed that he was the one Higgins had seen earlier. He might have been in charge of awakening the others.

"I am Motan Ylot, caretaker of the Micorites."

Tony Drake, standing beside Higgins, waited for the other to make some sort of greeting. Something as simple as a handshake had not been found in their literature or art. Finally, Motan Ylot raised a strange-looking hand. Tony mimicked the action, momentarily flustered due to the different arrangement of fingers, which brought a small smile to Motan Ylot's face. "I am Tony Drake, leader of the humans."

"If you know our language, you must know our history," said the Micorite.

"Some of it," Philbin said, then explaining who he was. "We know that a rogue star you named Borak entered your solar system, flinging some of the outer planets out into space, your world included. Before that occurred, you constructed these domed cities to protect your people against disturbances caused by Borak's approach. We didn't realize that the domes were meant to survive a voyage through open space and that your people still lived."

Hearing the talk turn to astrophysics as the linguist translated for Tony Drake, Duquesne made his way forward. "Your machines were automated to awaken you when they determined that the planet had reached a stable orbit, yes?"

With a puzzled expression at the sight of the ape-like Duquesne, Motan Ylot gestured with his head in a motion that the Earthmen decided meant "yes". He said, "It awoke a few of us, who were to decide if awakening every one of us was warranted or not. We spent weeks" – he used a Micorian measurement of time longer than a day but shorter than a month; since it depended on the planet's former orbit, the humans didn't use it, although they knew it – "studying the environment – and you humans."

"'Early Risers'," Duquesne offered.

Peter Vanderbilt exclaimed, "You've been taking our personal items – for study!"

Motan Ytol "nodded". "That is correct. We learned much from these items. You are a more materialistic, crasser people than we. But the decision of we three caretakers was that you would present no threat to us."

"Of course not," Tony exclaimed. Then he recalled the menace posed by the Asiatic alliance – and, he suddenly recalled Dave Ransdell's warning about the Italians. "Not all humans are peaceful. We are. We chose the best specimens of our race to survive the destruction of Earth. We hoped to establish a peaceful, progressive settlement here."

Motan Ytol "nodded" again. "Our calculations confirm that Micor's orbit is now stable, but eccentric."

Duquesne spoke up now, he being the expert on such topics. After explaining the units of measurement the humans used, he said, "We would be unable to survive the winter without the protection of your domes ... without migrating toward the equator, of course; which we would have to evacuate during the summer. The temperatures at this latitude range from one hundred fifty degrees to minus forty. Summer is now thirty-six days long, winter sixty-eight, spring and autumn fifty and fifty-one."

"Because of the extreme elongation of the orbit about your sun," mused Motan Ytol.

"Yes," confirmed the French physicist.

Tony Drake interjected, "There are only twelve hundred of us. We hope you will share your city with us."

"We cannot oppose it due to your numbers," answered the Micorite. "And we cannot exile you to your death as a race. However, our ruling council must discuss the topic."

"Of course," acknowledged Tony.

The humans watched as Motan Ytol returned to his duty. He spoke to those who were awake while the other two caretakers continued their job of awakening the remainder of the Other People.

After a few minutes, the eight Earthmen returned to the surface to inform the humans there, who, thus far, were blissfully unaware of what was occurring beneath their feet.

12

The Conquistador Syndrome

For the third time that day, Tony Drake interrupted the Re-Birth festivities, this time to announce that the Micorites were not dead, but merely slumbering, and that they were now awakening in the vault beneath Olympus-Gorfulu.

After a brief Central Authority meeting following the expedition to the vault, a small envoy was sent back to the awakening Micorites, in order to help facilitate their entry into the human camp. Everyone on the council was anxious about what would happen, and wanted to ensure good relations with the natives. Then they spent the rest of the Light Day planning for the coming emergence of the Micorites. Early the next Dark Day, Tony Drake made the announcement.

This was met by the expected surprise, apprehension and excitement. The throng of almost eleven hundred people was dead silent for a few moments, then the questions began. Tony called for quiet, and when he got it, he revealed all that he knew: The Micorites hadn't died, but gone into hibernation until their planet was capable of supporting life again. Now that it had, they were awakening. The Central Authority was in contact with them to ensure peaceful relations.

"There's nothing to worry about," he assured everyone who had gathered to hear him speak. "For the time being, the Micorites have no intention of displacing us. They want to live in peace and cooperation with us."

This news was met by cheering.

Following the annnouncment, Eliot James complained bitterly to Tony Drake that he should have been among thos who went to meet the natives, to record it for posterity.

Sheepishly, Tony explained, "I'm sorry, Eliot. It didn't occur to me. I was focused on the discovery and how to handle it, what it would mean for everyone if Higgins was correct."

The poet-cum-historian had to content himself with an audience with native representatives later, prior to a formal meeting between the two races.

The Re-Birth Day celebration took on a new tone, this one filled with excitement and trepidation in equal parts, when, that afternoon, the Micorites appeared. They had some idea what to expect, having been briefed both by the trio of caretakers, and the human envoy, as well. The Earthmen did their best to make them feel welcome.

Meanwhile, Dave Ransdell was set to arming the city's fleet of larks, in case the Italians should visit. Tony had decided against sending an envoy to Nova Italia, for surely they would be held prisoner as Dave had been. The idea of inviting a party from Nova Italia had been offered by Dodson, but the hazard was that any such party might act as spies. Even if they were cloistered, they might learn about the every day technology of the Micorites, and the Central Authority wanted to give the Italians no help in that regard.

After the Central Authority meeting, which had lasted for some time, one-armed Dodson returned to his hospital to continue work on finding a cure for the Sleeping Sickness. Days passed without any progress. The native plant pollen worked slightly differently than its Earth counterpart, not attacking the H1 receptor as expected.

Two Micorites entered the hospital, a man and a woman. The woman looked about, as if studying the place, while the male followed behind her. He gazed about with a curiosity that was less studious than the female's.

Dodson learned of their presence when an intern fetched him. He found the two visitors dressed very different from their first appearance, in what seemed to have been hospital gowns. These two were garbed in what appeared to be modern abstract art paintings put on cloth. To human eyes, the two garments, which were reminiscent of ancient Greek or Roman clothing in style, were eyesores.

The woman, whose hair was honey blonde, and quite long, said, "I am Anlas Nirol, and I am a doctor. I am here to help you with what you call 'the Sleeping Sickness'."

Dodson knew enough of the Micorian tongue – dubbed Micorese – to follow what was said, even if he didn't understand every word. When he glanced at the male Micorite, he received a puzzled look in return. Anlas Nirol looked at her companion and nodded, ever so slightly. The male said, "My name is Tobas Mylan."

"He is my *bilal*," explained Anlas Nirol.

"I see," murmured Dodson, not recognizing the word. "I am Dr. Charles Dodson."

"What progress have you made on treating the illness, Dr. Charles Dodson?" asked Anlas Nirol.

"We know it is an allergy to the pollen of certain native plants."

"Yes," nodded the Micorian doctor.

Tobas Mylan wandered about, investigating what he saw. He apparently had not seen many humans up close, and was intrigued by them. His expression was one of curiosity and fascination. The Micorite reached out to touch one of the interns, who happened to be female.

"Tobas!" Anlas Nirol called out sharply. The slave noticeably winced, seemingly in response to his name being called. Anlas Nirol's voice had been quite withering in tone.

"Are you all right?" Dodson said, hurrying over to the young man, who now appeared quite normal once again.

"He is all right," said Anlas Nirol. "I merely gave him a warning."

"I understand. But he seems to be in pain."

Anlas Nirol's pleasant face tightened. She seemed puzzled. "Of course. That was the warning."

It was Dodson's turn to be nonplussed. "What do you mean?"

"I sent him a short burst of mild pain to warn him to leave you humans alone. He is an excellent *bilal*, but a little too curious for his own good. He is especially intrigued by humans."

Dodson's perplexity deepened, which was signaled by his thick fingers tugging at his jawline whiskers. "You sent him pain?"

One of Anlas Nirol's slender fingers pointed to her head. "With my mind."

The Earth physician gasped. "You mean psychic ability!"

"What is that?" asked the Micorian woman.

Dodson briefly explained about psychic phenomenon on Earth, the tests conducted by J. B. Rhine using Zener cards, each of which contained one of five images: a circle, a cross, wavy lines, a square and a star. Rhine had published his findings the year catastrophe struck the Earth in the form of the first passage of the Bronson Bodies. With the nearing crisis, the work received little attention, except among a small, rabid following which believed that extra-sensory perception might hold the key to mankind's salvation. It hadn't.

"Some of us can see images in another's mind," said Anlas Nirol when Dodson had finished speaking. "Most of us can sense strong emotion, and all of us can influence the minds of others, in certain ways. It is quite common in love play."

"Does everyone possess it?" Dodson asked, incredulous.

"Everyone but *bilal*. We bred it out of them millennia ago, to protect ourselves." Then, seemingly bored with the topic, Anlas Nirol said, "We possess the cure for your Sleeping Sickness. It has the same effect upon us, but it is not fatal. Probably, it is fatal to humans due to your slightly different biology."

"Yes, yes," Dodson, agreed, nodding his head slowly, unable to forget Micorian psychic ability. "You said that this ability had been bred out of *bilal*. What do you mean?"

Anlas Nirol explained that "bilal" was the Micorian word for what Earthmen called a slave, but it was somewhat subtler than that. It was closer in meaning to indentured servant. *Bilal* was a station in life, like watchmaker, a term that denoted both function and class, not merely human property as it did on Earth.

Dodson hmmm-ed in disapproval. He opposed slavery in all its forms. But he was wise enough to admit that he did not know much about the alien culture, and could not fully condemn the practice. Certainly, it was better than multitudes of people received on Earth, both in the distant past and even the present. "Well," he said in a resigned tone, for nothing he could say to the Micorian woman would alter the natiuve culture or its practices, "perhaps we should discuss the Sleeping Sickness."

"I will show you the chemical compound to prevent attacks by the allergy," said Dr. Anlas Nirol.

Weeks passed as the Micorites integrated into human society – or rather, vice-versa, as the Earth colonists were greatly outnumbered. Ten million natives stayed mainly in Olympus-Gorfulu, it being the capital of the five cities, while the rest, which numbered about half the total of those who had awakened, distributed themselves unevenly among Wend, the westernmost city, Strahl, in the north, and Danot, to the east. Hendron-Khorlu they were content to leave as a farm city for everyone. The Micorites were intrigued by human cuisine.

There were ten such hubs on this continent, which was called Nurustruhl, and contained four major nations and wilderness areas near the polar regions which had been inhabited by primitives and those rejecting the strictures of society. There were three major nations on Borealis, one of which had moved its populace underground; other nations had developed their own plans for surviving Borak's passing, including the building of an ark like the ones humans had used to settle on Bronson Beta. While the planet shared a common culture, there were many subcultures, each with its own dialect. And although everyone understood the written language, the dialects were so varied that people from one nation could not always understand another when speaking.

The humans learned that while the Micorites were indeed enlightened, their culture had its dark side: They kept slaves. This was not based on race, as it was on Earth, but on nationality. Before war had ended on Micor, citizens of warring nations were taken as slaves and belonged to a recognized caste in society. When peace finally came, slavery did not end.

Before Borak had arrived, Micorian society progressed to the point where little manual labor was required, and what there was of it was done by the slaves. Since machines did the backbreaking work, slaves tended to be of a more personal nature, handmaids or valets, who did things like lay out clothes for their master or mistress and do the daily shopping. Chefs were especially prized. Generally, as a class, *bilal* were well treated.

And then the humans learned about the Games.

13

The Games of Nurustruhl

The Earthmen knew of the Games. Each of the five cities had a stadium filled with grass, surrounded by seats. The one in Olympus-Gorfulu was the largest of these. They had been playing baseball in it, while the one in Hendron-Khorlu was being used to grow fresh fruit and vegetables throughout the winter.

The humans even knew something of the sport, which was called Chaclac. Each team propelled a ball down the field by striking it. Any body part could be used to hit the ball – hand, foot, even head – everything was fair game. Holding or even grabbing it was forbidden. This was somewhat like European football, known in the

United States as soccer, except that there were no goalies. Leaving a man to guard the scoring area was optional; there was no special station for him as in soccer and hockey, and such a guard possessed no special privileges.

The goal was a stone with a hole in it atop a pedestal; a score was made by passing the ball through the hole in the stone ring. The use of stone rather than some newer, manufactured material attested to the antiquity of the game. The stone goals in the stadium in Olympus-Gorfulu were said to have been the first ever used when Chaclac was created. A fiction to be sure, but a harmless one.

Micorites, armed with small colored flags and short metallic sticks which resembled drumsticks, filled the stadium on game day. Attendees wore scarves of either red or gold, the colors of Micor and the colors of the two opposing teams. There were, of course, too few seats for the great population that had awakened, and the remainder watched the game on flat cathode ray tubes set in cabinets. Pierre Duquesne had recognized these as advanced television apparatus, which had just been invented a few years before the Bronson bodies had been sighted. The Frenchman had explained their operation to his fellow Earthmen early on, and the devices came into use in Hendron-Khorlu. While no entertainment programs could be found in the Micorian records – these would have been quite revealing, Duquesne though! – the humans were able to access libraries full of educational shows. These were intended for the teaching of children, or manuals on how to re-start civilization, not unlike the paper library Cole Hendron's people had brought to Bronson Beta.

Dramatic march-like music filled the air as two teams, each consisting of five men, entered the field, one in gold uniforms and the other in red. These two hues were national colors, apparently, like the red, white and blue of the United States. The gold uniforms were trimmed in black, and the red in white. The secondary colors seemed to have no significance other than visual appeal.

Each of the two teams formed in a diamond pattern, with one man in the center of the quadrangle. The lead man on each team was positioned near the center of the field, where the ball rested on the short, green grass. This had been prepared for the game, trimmed very short in order not to impede the progress of the ball. It was also lightly wetted with some sort of oily liquid that would allow the players to slide in the grass without friction burning their flesh, but did not hinder running. Rudolf Neuberg, a German socialist chemist who also happened to be a European football fan and thus watching the Game with some Micorites, was fascinated by the subtlety of the concoction when told about it.

The beginning signal sounded and the game began. Everyone rushed forward toward the ball, except the rear player on the gold team. He stayed behind to guard the goal. The red team chose to deploy a single player at same end of the field, in case the ball could be sent to him, leaving their own goal undefended.

This tactic proved fortuitous, for the red team got control of the ball, and quickly passed it down field. The forward man used his body to block the gold player from intercepting the ball as a red confederate knocked it into the stone ring, scoring the first goal of the game.

Play stopped as the ball was returned to its starting position in the center of the field by one of three neutral figures who were the equivalent of referees. They wore black, and treated as if they didn't exist – until they cried "foul!" – like the *kuroko* stagehands in Japanese No theater. The ten players returned to their starting positions, taking their time so that they could catch their breath.

Red once again got control of the ball – their forward man was quite fast – but quickly lost it as the ball was intercepted by a gold man as the forward shot it down the field to a teammate. He passed it along to his nearest teammate and ran interference for him all the way to the goal, where the ball was blocked by a red player who swooped in, using the special lubricant on the field to slide some twenty feet for the interception.

The crowd leapt to their feet to applaud the play – by banging their two sticks together that resembled drumsticks. These were hollow, which increased the volume of the beating. The clatter was deafening for several moments.

The ball ricocheted between two players and flew out of bounds, causing it to be returned to its starting position. By the time this was done, the stick clattering had faded away.

This time, gold took possession of the ball, and quickly moved it down the field. They were a more cautious team, and kept control of the ball as the red players dogged their heels. Like a team of surgeons, they worked together with precise moves to score a goal.

Everyone returned to their starting positions.

The final score, after three fifteen-minute terms, separated by five minute rest periods, was 3-2 gold, their more cautious method of play winning out over the more risky and reckless strategy of the red team.

A literal feast followed the game, attended by the players, who were the honorees, and Micorite officials, all of whom who virtually unknown to the Earthmen. Micorian society seemed to function largely without leaders. The officials could best be described as administrators, not ministers.

Pierre Duquesne, who possessed a highly inquisitive mind as well as enjoying a good meal, finagled an invitation to the feast. He was respected by the Micorites for his brilliant brain. When he noticed that the losing red team seemed to be getting the lion's share of attention, he asked his neighbor at the table, "Why are the members of the red team being so honored? On Earth, only the winners are celebrated."

"Because this is their last meal," said the Micorite fellow in a non-chalant tone.

"What do you mean?" asked the Frenchman, puzzled.

"The losers are put to death after their tribute."

"What?!" thundered Duquesne. "What do you mean?"

"If they have nothing to lose, what will impel them to play their best?" queried the man beside Duquesne.

"You mean they will be executed for losing?" the Frenchman asked incredulously.

"It is a great honor to play, and the men die honored as heroes," explained the fellow. "No one wants to die, of course, but dying for the Games is the most honorable way to die, to have been selected to play in the first place.

"The players are normally all *bilal*," said Duquesne's neighbor. "But the greatest player of all time was a free man who gave up his freedom for love of the Game."

"*Incroyable!*" exclaimed Duquesne, reverting to his native tongue without realizing it.

The human colonists, who were unaware of this gruesome fact about the Micorian Game, did not know the players had been killed until Dark Day.

The day after the sacrifices had been made, Notor Piyel, a Micorian male, went mad and attacked a number of people on the streets of Olympus-Gorfulu.

14

The Human Strain

Dr. Charles Dodson, Dr. Harold Runciman, the brain specialist, and Anlas Nirol consulted on the case of Notor Piyel after examining him. Dr. Smith, Chief of Surgery, was also present in a consulting capacity. The Micorian doctor had used the technology of her people to study her patient. There was no talk of the execution of the red team players. The human doctors were used to compartmentalizing their feelings, separating emotions from work, and now they were focused on the medical problem at hand.

"This illness is unknown to us," pronounced Anlas Nirol, her pleasant face tight with puzzlement.

"You don't have mental illness here?" Dr. Runciman asked in an incredulous tone.

"I mean that Notor Piyel does not have any known disease, despite his obvious symptoms," explained Anlas Nirol. "I can sense his turmoil."

"Could it be some sort of *psychic* illness?" Dodson ventured. "Perhaps caused by your long hibernation?"

"Perhaps," mused the Micorian woman in a skeptical tone. She was plainly puzzled.

"I'm not a virologist but I have to wonder if it's not an Earth disease," offered Runciman. "The Micorites may react differently to it just as we humans do their plant allergy."

"I'd considered that," responded Dodson, "but his symptoms are at odds with such a diagnosis, in my opinion. In the case of the allergy, humans had the same symptoms as the Micorites, but much more severely."

"True."

"What do you suggest we do, doctor?" Dodson asked the Micorian physician.

Anlas Nirol glanced first at Notor Piyel then at the two humans. "Keep him restrained and calm, while I consult the medical libraries."

Dodson and Runciman watched as the lovely woman departed. Dodson said, "Another reason I rule out a virus is that there's no pattern to what happened to Notor Piyel. If it was a virus, why aren't there more cases? Why now, after weeks of contact between the two races?"

Runciman scratched his balding scalp thoughtfully. "You know, Charles ... I've heard some of the interns talking. Some of our fellow humans have been having ... relations ... with some of the Micorites."

"Relations?" ejaculated the salt-and-pepper-haired physician as what his colleague had said sunk in. He had no inkling of this.

"Syphilis can cause dementia."

"But tertiary syphilis takes a minimum of three years to develop," countered Dodson.

"In humans," corrected Runciman. "What if Micorites react to social diseases the way humans react to pollen allergy here?"

"Well, a simple blood test should tell us the answer," Dodson said with finality.

Notor Piyel did not have syphilis, nor any other Earth disease that could be identified by a blood test. The two human physicians had run the entire gamut of tests, on the theory that the Micorite's body might be reacting differently to an Earth illness than a human's would. Of course, this did not rule out many other illnesses that could not be detected by a simple blood test. So the two doctors were once again stymied.

They had performed these tests before Anlas Nirol returned from her own studies. Frustrated at their lack of progress, Dodson finally said, "Your theory about a social disease has me thinking. Something makes this man different. Perhaps if we can learn what he did in the days before his violent episode, we can find something."

"Something he did that no others did."

Dodson nodded. "Let us see if we can find someone who can investigate Notor Piyel's last days for us."

"I'll go to the Safety office this afternoon," offered Runciman. The Micorite was technically *his* patient.

"No, no," Dodson objected. "Nothing so formal. And no one there has been trained as an investigator. For all their value and service, they are – no disrespect intended – merely muscle men. I have heard there is some sort of policeman among the British. Perhaps even more than one."

After a number of discreet inquiries, Dodson and Runciman found their man: Nicholas Caswell. "Nicky", as his friends called him, was relatively young for one who had accomplished so much. He had been a flying ace during the Great War, and, afterward, a policeman, eventually joining Scotland Yard and finally becoming an Inspector shortly before Sven Bronson's life-changing discovery in 1931. He was now thirty-five years old, old Earth-style reckoning. It was difficult for everyone to think of their ages in new measurements, and so they didn't.

Physically, Nicky was thin but in trim shape. With watery blue eyes and thinning blond hair, he vaguely resembled the actor Leslie Howard, whose last role was the film "Of Human Bondage", released on the eve of the first passage of the Bronson planets. It had made Bette Davis famous for all of a week. Then everyone had more urgent things to think about.

That was the last year films were released. 1934 marked the end of human civilization, even if the Bronson twins had not returned the following year. Between the volcanism produced by the passage of the two planets and the resulting tsunamis, civilization had been wiped out. It could have been re-built, a process that would likely have taken decades, if Earth had not been destroyed the next year.

The two doctors found Caswell to be mild-mannered, but he asked the right questions, and they realized his timid exterior belied a keen mind. Once he understood his assignment – which he welcomed, not having had the opportunity to practice his vocation since the destruction of the Earth – Nicky Caswell set about his task. Several days later, he returned with his report.

By this time, Anlas Nirol had announced that she could find no Micorian disease that fit the patient's symptoms – none other than insanity; that is, none of a strictly medical nature, and the three physicians were forced to conclude that Notor Piyel's problem was located in his brain and solely in his brain. Anlas Nirol was reluctant to operate, with so little to go on, and wanted to conduct further tests of a more complicated and lengthy nature.

During this period, another Micorite went berserk – this time a woman, Aro Ylar. A third had a violent breakdown before Nicky Caswell made his report. Notor Piyel had indeed had sexual relations with an Earth woman. As far as the Englishman could determine, Notor Piyel had done nothing else unusual in the weeks before his attack, had not eaten anything no one else had, had not visited any site no one else had. His life had been like any other Micorite, except for his relationship with the Earth woman Starla Mason.

Dodson immediately said, "We have two more for you to look into, Mr. Caswell."

"Nicky," corrected the Englishman in a friendly tone. "Give me their names and I'll do my best." He then went about his new assignment, happy to have found new purpose.

When three more Micorites fell ill under similar circumstances, Charles Dodson went to Tony Drake.

The young stockbroker appeared more nervous than usual when he stood before the human settlers, who numbered something over eleven hundred; even those in the satellite cities had been called in to attend the announcement. Every able-bodied Earthman and Earthwoman was present. They had been summoned to one of the buildings still occupied by the Earthmen, which had been used for such meetings in previous months. It had been a music hall, with a great instrument not unlike a pipe organ, and was currently Marlene Dietrich's theater.

Beside Tony stood Dr. Charles Dodson and Dr. Anlas Nirol, who had agreed that this was a necessary step in determining the cause of the Micorian outbreaks, even if she wasn't convinced it was accurate. Sometimes you learned what "was" by ruling out what "was not".

Tony Drake raised his hands to signal for silence. "What I have to say may be indelicate, but I assure you, it's of the utmost importance. So I'm going to ask for your indulgence. Suspend your judgment so that we can solve the problem."

A murmur ran through the crowd. Whatever the topic was, it sounded important.

Finally, the humans settled down enough that Tony could continue.

"Our medical experts have a theory what is causing the mental breakdowns of those few Micorites who have recently gone berserk. They believe that they may be contracting an illness from we Earthmen."

Another murmur, this one louder. Now there was something to discuss. Tony let this go on for a few moments, then waved his hands over his head again, and called out, "Please!"

This had the desired effect, and he began to speak once more. "It looks possible that the disease is spread through contact with humans ... contact of a certain nature. I want to stress that those involved do not have a disease, per se. We believe that the Micorites may be reacting to a harmless Earth disease the way some humans react to pollen allergy here on Bronson Beta.

"I want to repeat this: Please suspend your judgment ... I don't want any aspersions cast upon anyone here. If they are singled out for ridicule or moral judgment, they may be reluctant to be forthcoming with the information we need to confirm or dispute this proposed theory.

"And that's all it is now – a theory."

More murmurings. Tony let this die down of its own accord. He wanted everyone paying full attention to what he had to say next.

Tony Drake was more concerned about the newcomers – the Europeans and the Asians. The American contingent had been chosen carefully, and they knew that a new morality would be in play on Bronson Beta. There were no religious fanatics among them. He knew that they could handle the news. The former stockbroker wasn't so sure about the others.

"It's come to my attention that some of us have been … intermingling with the Micorites. The doctors believe that an Earth disease may be spread in this way."

Another murmur. This one was louder than the others, and showed no signs of dying down. A number of eyes shot toward Marian Jackson, who had been a dancer in St. Louis, and was known to have been free with her affections before settling down with Peter Vanderbilt, and a number of other women who were thought of as "loose". Plural marriage was an inevitable fact of life on Bronson Beta, while bed-hopping was still disapproved of by many, particularly those of the older generation. Those who had been young during the Roaring Twenties were more accepting of relaxed morality.

Tony Drake broke in, yelling above the noise. "Everyone, quiet!"

Then, in a more reasonable volume, "We're all adults here. We know what adults do together. We had to abandon Earth morality to re-start the human race here. This is no time for coyness or fake outrage. I'm not talking about social diseases. We think it's possible that diseases, say, like polio, or even the common cold, may be spread through contact with the Micorites.

"What we need is for everyone who has had such intimate contact with a Micorite report to the hospital in the next day. We need to make a list of Micorites who might be infected. If those who have had breakdowns are not on that list, we can then rule out this theory, and look for a new one.

"I'm not going to tolerate gossip or shaming of anyone who comes forward," pronounced Tony Drake loudly and firmly. This left no doubt as to his feelings about the subject. "Is that clear?"

A wave of murmurs went through the crowd. It was such a clamor that it was impossible to determine its tone. When it died down, the young leader of Olympus-Gorfulu said, "I know you may be embarrassed, but if you have had contact with a Micorite, please come forward. It may be the key to cracking this illness, and your medical record is confidential, just as it was on Earth. The hospital will be open day and night. Come at your convenience.

"All right, that's all."

Tony Drake turned to the two doctors who stood with him as the crowd began to disperse, noisily filing out of the amphitheater. Dodson nodded his approval of the young man's speech.

"Let's hope it does some good," Tony smiled wanly, glancing at his wife. Eve's slender face was unreadable. Her grandfather had been a minister, so she understood that side of the opinions that were forming even now in the throng. But she had grown up in the Roaring Twenties, and, although a little too young to have been a flapper, also understand the relaxed morals of her generation. She herself had argued that Earth morality might have to fall by the wayside in order to make society function on a new world. Marriage, for example, had reverted to polygamy, in order to address the imbalance between the sexes. But old mores were hard to shake loose, Eve knew.

Anlas Nirol interrupted the couple's gaze. She seemed puzzled. "You humans' attitude toward sexual congress is most unnatural."

Neither Tony nor Dodson had any response to that. The Micorian system of marriage was completely unlike that of any on Earth. Marriages were between friends, a male and female who were compatible. They did not have a sexual relationship. Each sought that kind of affection and satisfaction outside of marriage, and, since there was no passionate love between the spouses, there was no jealousy over this practice.

Eliot James stroked his small beard as he contemplated his diary. It read:

> This latest problem highlights the differences between our two races.
>
> The Micorites are so like us, and yet so unlike us. They strongly resemble us physically – or rather, we they, since their race is far older than out own – the major differences being the placement of their thumbs – and large toes – on the outside of their appendages, an enlarged area of the

brain which seems to be the source of their extra-sensory powers, and the distribution of certain organs in their abdomens.

Their emotional range seems somewhat limited compared to that of we humans, though it is unclear whether the cause of this is biological or cultural. They seem to be more open with their feelings among themselves. This has caused some Earthmen to suggest they are shy around us, strangers in their home, but Dr. Dodson thinks it is something else.

The hardest thing for us to accept is their slavery, which is not as awful as it first seemed. Unlike the slaves we know from American history, Micorian slavery is not based on race, and the *bilal* possess certain rights. There were other ways to become a slave, other than being born one, it turns out: to pay a debt, or as punishment for a crime. The Micorites built no prisons. Murderers could volunteer to become slaves, to be spared execution. *Bilal* could buy their freedom, or be released if they could show they'd been mistreated by their master. If they either married, or had children with, their master, this also freed them. *Bilal* could not be sold without their consent. A certain type of slave, best translated as "incorrigible", lost these rights.

Worst of all is the barbaric Games – but the *bilal* participate freely, even enthusiastically, so most of our race remains silent on the topic, out of respect for a culture we don't fully understand. I suspect the silence of some is due to the fact that we are guests, and we reside in their domed cities at their pleasure. We would either have to migrate south for the winter, or die in the extreme cold, if we annoyed them enough to cause them to force us to leave their cities.

But the Micorites seem to enjoy our presence, as if we were wild animals who settled down in their camp. We are welcome company and they are curious about as – as much as we are about them. Will they come to view us as pets? Do they already?

At the end of fifty hours, over a dozen people had come forward, some Americans, some Europeans and some Asians. A list was compiled of those who had had intimate contact with a Micorite and was being cross referenced when a group of lark ships appeared in the spring sky over Olympus-Gorfulu.

15

Assault on Olympus

In Olympus-Gorfulu, panic ensued. The populace had been told of the Italian settlement, but their presence at the domed city came as a surprise. Some in the Central Authority had expected – and dreaded – this day. Some civilians, such as Eliot James, who possessed some understanding of history and politics but particularly of human nature, was not shocked at the sight of the Italian planes, only surprised by it.

Most of the human populace ran for cover, despite the transparent metal of the dome being virtually impenetrable. The Micorites, a somewhat more subdued people, were, as usual, less demonstrative of their emotions, whatever they were. They had constructed the dome to withstand the ravages of deep space and time, and knew it to be impervious to Earth technology. They expressed feelings of concern and puzzlement over the attack, not terror.

Overhead, the larks buzzed like angry hornets. They had been re-painted, and now bore the colors of il Tricolore, the Italian flag, green, white, and red. Featured prominently on each side was painted an eagle clutching a fasces, the symbol of fascism.

But a more deadly change had been made to the little planes: The Italians had mounted machine guns on them. The pilots strafed the few vehicles that were on the metal-like roads that ran between the cities. Essentially built from sheet metal, these offered little protection for their occupants, despite the durability of Micorian steel.

The Italians in the larks did not waste their ammunition against the dome; they knew better. Doubtless, they had conducted experiments on Micorian metal in the weeks since they'd discovered the domed city in the west.

Peter Vanderbilt activated the volunteer defense brigade, which basically consisted of every able-bodied man – *hu*man – in Olympus-Gorfulu. There had been no talk of incorporating Micorites into the brigade, for they'd had no army, and there was no imminent threat. It was not even known if they *would* fight, if pressed.

Looking at each of his lieutenants – Jack Little, Bill Whittington, and Eric Leeds – the New Yorker told them, "Each of you take a gate. Round up as many men as you can to go with you – at least a couple dozen. Arm no more than that many." A multitude of individuals was waiting outside the Safety Office, ready to fulfill their duty, but there were only so many firearms to go around, and Peter wanted to make sure that these were evenly distributed amongst the gates.

"What about the other gates?" asked young Bill. There were eight such portals in the city.

"I have men in mind to defend those. Don't worry. Just go!" With that, Peter went into an anteroom, where four others waited. These were Dave Ransdell, Pierre Duquesne, Kyto and Jack Taylor, who, as Tony Drake's aide-de-camp, had been dispatched to gather the others as soon as the air raid alarm sounded following the sighting of the green, white and red larks; this was a short series of musical notes played upon one of the great instruments in the music hall, piped throughout the city so that all heard it. This system had been set up shortly after Olympus-Gorfulu had been settled, as a catchall for any emergency. No one expected it would be used as an air raid siren warning of an attack by fellow Earthmen. A natural disaster had been on the minds of the Central Authority members when they'd thought it up.

Pierre Duquesne, as if reading the young redhead's mind, had assured him, "I fought in the trenches in the Great War. I'm not so old I can't still fight." A true patriot, the Frenchman had not been a young man when the Great War started in 1914. He was now fifty-one years old.

Peter Vanderbilt quickly assigned these four to certain gates. In fact, he trusted them more than most of his own police force, since most of this quartet had all seen action in war. Peter himself would man the eighth gate. Although Tony Drake had volunteered to lead one of the defense groups, he was flatly turned down. He was too important as leader of the Olympus-Gorfulu, and he knew this himself. Such was his commitment to his people that he wanted to fight for them personally. Tony was brave, and a born fighter.

While groups moved to the gates, smaller units went to intersections and directed traffic, keeping people moving, or getting them off the streets to allow those that wished to pass to do so. Everyone who could was heading for cover, for, although there seemed to be no imminent danger, human nature feared the unknown.

Tensions were high in the city as the green, white and red hornets buzzed overhead. Some of the wiser residents knew that the flying tactics of the Italians were to cause terror, but this did little to calm nerves. And there were too many who did not understand this. Panic filled the carefully controlled atmosphere of Olympus-Gorfulu.

The Micorites, as a group, appeared unconcerned. For what could a few men of an inferior race to do them? They had constructed the dome. They knew its capability. They felt no fear.

The natives of Bronson Beta were more interested in the behavior of their new neighbors. The humans possessed the same information as the Micorites, yet they were afraid. It was most puzzling. Seeing the mad panic with which the Earthmen moved about Olympus-Gorfulu, many of the Micorites were motivated to vacate the streets for their own safety. They moved to observe the proceedings from the safety of their homes.

Men stood ready at every gate, for this was the only known way into the domed city. Even if, by some miracle, the dome were damaged, the Italians would still have to launch a ground assault to take the city. While the fear of the unknown gripped many of the defenders, many were filled with optimism: There were fewer Italians than there were humans in Olympus-Gorfulu – no more than three hundred, according to Dave Ransdell's account – and the defenders had the advantage.

The men who had experienced combat had mixed feelings. It made no sense for the Italians to mount an assault that was doomed to fail. Therefore, they must have believed they had found a way to penetrate the city's defense.

Dave Ransdell, standing at his assigned gate, watched the larks buzzing overhead. He wished that Olympus-Gorfulu's own planes were equipped with guns, so that he could take a squadron up and drive off the Italians.

He laughed inwardly. Sending his planes back to him full of holes would show the brazen Mussolini! But it was not to be.

Suddenly, the rumble of thunder echoed throughout the city. Dave's robin's-egg blue eyes narrowed as he watched the green, white and red larks – their pattern of flight had changed. They were strafing the dome!

Dave knew the sound of machine gun fire. This wasn't that. It was some other type of weapon.

And then it hit him – the Italians had developed some sort of gun using Micorian technology! Perhaps the dome could be breached, after all. Man had yet to create something that he could not destroy. The Micorites might easily be the same.

Screams filled the climate-controlled air. The general populace now realized what Dave knew: The Italians were attacking the dome.

Dave studied the transparent metal above. It was difficult to determine if the Italians' slugs – whatever they were – were having any effect. The zenith of the dome was a mile up, too distant to see if holes were being created by the constant thrumming of bullets. Unless the Italians planned to use gas, such insignificant damage would make no difference. Even gas would be difficult to aim properly through such small apertures. There had to be another motive for the strafing.

The big South African waited and watched but nothing happened. He concluded that the Italians using their guns against the dome was nothing more than another terror tactic, designed to frighten the residents of Olympus-Gorfulu into submission.

Well, it wouldn't work. There were too many who would fight for their freedom. Dave Ransdell knew that. Although there were no soldiers among the Argonauts – that is, none chosen for their fighting skill – there were plenty like himself and Tony Drake and Pierre Duquesne who would fight for Olympus-Gorfulu, regardless of their experience or skill.

Then, a great ship appeared in the sky over the mountains to the west. Then another, and another.

The Micorites had built planes other than the single passenger larks. A number of these sat in hangars on the small airfield in Olympus-Gorfulu, and the other Micorian cities. These larger craft had first become known when troops of the Asiatic alliance used them to invade the original campsite of the smaller American ark. The Earthmen used these, sometimes, but not greatly. Rarely was such a large vessel needed. Survey teams and expeditions used them, but no one else.

The big transports began to land on the flat earth of the vast plain around the dome. The men stationed at the gates watched as uniformed soldiers began pouring from the ships. There were dozens of them, perhaps hundreds.

The word went out: A ground assault was coming!

16

Invasion!

Like an inexorable army of ants, the Italian troops came forward, splitting into two groups as they neared the wall of the dome, one for each of the two gates facing west – the gates sat at the points of a St. George's Cross, so there were two for each cardinal direction. These were the North Wend Gate and the South Wend Gate, Wend being the Micorian city that lay to the southwest some two hundred miles. The eight gates of the city were named for the four cities that surrounded Olympus-Gorfulu, one at each cardinal point, roughly.

Despite the protection of the dome, the soldiers, garbed in crisp new uniforms woven from fabric of Bronson Beta, were a frightening sight. The battle suddenly became real to all those men who believed that the impenetrability of Olympus-Gorfulu's dome would force an Italian retreat. This was plainly not the case.

Would the gates repel the invaders?

The gates of the Micorian cities, as constructed, were not fortified. Like any portal, they possessed latches. These were a bit complicated, and would foil, for a time, anyone attempting to use them from the outside. However, they were not locks, but merely fasteners, and once one knew how to open such a fastener, all were then easy to open. Knowing this, the humans in Olympus-Gorfulu had reinforced the gates upon hearing Dave Ransdell's story; that the Italians had figured out how to unfasten the gates, knew where Olympus-Gorfulu was, and had transportation to get there – the colorfully painted larks.

From the great belly of one of the transport ships emerged a machine unlike any those in Olympus-Gorfulu had seen before. Smaller than a family automobile and rather boxy looking, this was guided by two of the Italians toward the nearest city gate.

The Italian men who were mobbed around the gate – they were chanting and yelling at the defenders of the city while waving their guns menacingly – parted to allow the odd machine through. It somewhat resembled a mechanical street sweeper in size and shape, though lacked the whirling brushes.

The Earthmen inside the gate watched nervously, not knowing what to expect. They readied their weapons, which had come from Earth.

The Italians pushed the machine up to the gate, which was defended by Eric Leeds. He'd been chosen by Peter Vanderbilt to defend the gate most likely to be attacked – the South Wend Gate, since it was literally the gate nearest the city of the Italians – because he had military experience in ground warfare. As a young man, he'd fought in the trenches in France in the Great War. He had left England an idealistic boy and returned a cynical man.

Not that he regretted fighting in the war. It had to be done. The Central Powers were gobbling up Europe. The Gordian Knot of treaties in Europe had led to the entire world becoming entangled in war. If it had not been so tragic, it would have been funny.

But young Eric had become disabused of the notion that there was anything noble about war. It was awful, despite its necessity. It was the very definition of "necessary evil". He had come to the conclusion that no one should initiate war for any reason. The only valid reason to go to war was defense, to stop an attack on itself or to stop some other nation in its war on another country.

At forty, Eric Leeds was the second oldest of the quartet of peacekeepers of Olympus-Gorfulu, being but a few years younger than the leader of the security force.

That was how he liked to think of them, as keepers of the peace, rather than as policemen who solved crimes. There was not much crime in the city, and Eric was no detective. He liked keeping the peace, doing so in a peaceful manner. He was no head-cracker or skull-buster. But when the Italians came, he was happy to assume responsibility for the defense of one of the eight gates of Olympus-Gorfulu. Sometimes violence was necessary, and defense of one's self, property, livelihood, or loved ones was just cause for it.

Clicks and clacks emanated from the portal as Eric Leeds watched the Italians work. The machine was doing something. He couldn't see what – the gate itself blocked his view. Slowly, realization of what was occurring dawned on the soldiers of Olympus-Gorfulu: The machine was unlocking the fortified fastener of the gate! The Italians were breaching the dome!

"Ready, men!" Eric Leeds called out. "They're coming in!"

As the gate began to open, the Brit yelled, "Go warn the others!" One of the unarmed reserve volunteers ran to do as he was instructed.

Bullets flew thick as the invaders fought their way in through the aperture when it was finally fully open. The fighting was bloody, savage.

The defenders had the advantage in that the gate created a bottleneck that the invaders had to fight their way through. The Greeks had faced a similar challenge at Thermopylae. The Argonauts suffered the same problem: overwhelming odds. There were simply too many of the Italians for the small number of armed defenders, who were outnumbered at near five to one at South Wend Gate. Inch by inch, foot by foot, the invaders came through the portal.

Bodies piled up at the gateway, creating another obstacle for the invaders. Blood slickened the avenue inside the gate. It was as sickening a sight as any who had fought in the Great War had seen. Ten Italians died for every soldier of Olympus-Gorfulu at the bottleneck. But there were so many of them, and they were better armed.

It was not that the Italian men outnumbered the American, British, German, Russian and Japanese men – no, they were actually fewer of them. But there were far more Italian *soldiers* – almost every male in Nova Italia was a soldier, while the other factions had not brought so many weapons. The unarmed volunteers of the domed city waited, behind cover, until one of their fellows fell, then rushed forward, scooping up their comrade's weapon, and took up the fight.

Finally, once the Italians had broken through, Dimitri Kalov, one of the Americans, urged his fellow citizens forward, despite being unarmed. There were enough volunteer reservists, he reasoned, to overwhelm the numerically inferior Italian force. A number of men followed him forward. The Russian émigré, who had fled communist Russia after the October Revolution, was gunned down leading his impromptu charge, which failed as wave after wave of unarmed men fell to Italian bullets.

Casualties flooded into Olympus-Gorfulu's small hospital. The space had not been chosen for its expansive size, for there were few injuries or illnesses in Olympus-Gorfulu. Its four beds were never full. There had never been more than one or two inpatients – until the Sleeping Sickness struck again.

It wasn't long before nearby rooms were commandeered to handle the overflow of patients coming in from the battle. Most who made it to the hospital needed only minor treatment, and, once given, they were moved to a resting chamber in an adjacent building. The more serious cases filled the operating room, causing two makeshift O.R.s to be established in addition to the existing one.

Charles Dodson and his staff were overwhelmed. Numerous women had volunteered to help. Though possessing no medical training, they could staunch minor bleeding and render comfort to the wounded. Dodson, unable to perform surgery with only one arm, oversaw the activities of the volunteers. Even with all the extra help, there were simply not enough qualified medical personnel or facilities to handle all the injured.

And the battle had just begun. Things were going to get infinitely worse before they got better.

This same bloody battle scene was repeated at the North Wend Gate.

Kyto, formerly Tony Drake's manservant, had been assigned this portal. Unknown to the stockbroker until after the migration to Bronson Beta, the Japanese man had actually been a spy for his government, sent to watch the United States. Kyto had enlisted in the Imperial Japanese Army – more accurately translated as the "Army of the

Great Japanese Empire" – as a teenager. Romantic nationalism was sweeping through Japan in the late 1920s, and young Kyto had been swept along with most of his countrymen. As a result of this movement, the Army became the Imperial Army in 1928.

Kyto – whose full name was Mifune Kyto – had showed intelligence and an aptitude for espionage work and was quickly transferred to military intelligence. After a suitable training period, he was sent to New York City, where he became the employee of Tony Drake, who possessed connections to many of America's financial elite. He acted as valet, chauffeur and, when needed, bodyguard.

By this time, Japan had invaded Manchuria, re-naming it Manchukuo, and the country's military was anxious to know how the United States would react to their expansion into mainland Asia. Japan had been forced out of Siberia by the U.S. after the Great War. Hokushin-ron ("Northern Road") was a Japanese doctrine that called for expansion into and development of Manchuria and Siberia, as buffers against the Soviet Union; these areas also presented Japan with economic opportunities far superior to any other nearby region.

The arrival of the Bronson planets in 1931 cut short every nation's military plans, including Japan's. It, too, attempted constructing an ark, but the country's technology was not up to it, and the craft failed upon takeoff, killing everyone aboard, including Emperor Hirohito, the royal family, and Admiral Yamamoto, who had been in charge of the project, which had fallen under the purview of the Imperial Japanese Navy.

By this time, Kyto was firmly ensconced in America, and his loyalties had shifted to the Americans, having experienced their way of life firsthand for a number of years. With his military experience – only the broadest sense of which had been revealed to anyone other than Tony Drake – he was a natural choice to defend one of the Wend Gates.

The Italian soldiers pushed through the mass of corpses that lay at their feet just inside the North Wend Gate, after the lock picking machine had been applied to the gate's fastener as it had been to the south. It didn't matter which side the bodies belonged to – if either. Being dead, they belonged only to eternity, some would say. Little by little, the invaders entered Olympus-Gorfulu.

Kyto signaled a retreat – only thus could he hope to stop the Italian advance by re-grouping with fresh reinforcements. His own force had been decimated by the advancing Italian soldiers, who, once inside the bottleneck aperture, proved too much for the city's defenders.

Kyto aligned his troops along the main avenue that led toward the center of Olympus-Gorfulu, expecting the invaders to move to take control of the vital sections of the city. But once inside the North Wend Gate, they did something unexpected.

The Italians did not take time to rejoice, nor hesitate uncertainly. The soldiers began to move, shooting down any resistance, toward the South Wend Gate. The two portals invaded were near one another, about a mile apart, and the Italian force re-grouped near the southernmost of the two gates. The city defenders at the South Wend Gate were mowed down from behind, surprised by the secondary Italian force from the North Wend gate. Eric Leeds was among those who were ambushed and killed.

A blood bath ensued as Americans, Brits, Germans, Russians and Japanese stormed forward to retrieve abandoned weapons. They were cut down in wave after wave, until, finally, there were no more reinforcements waiting. Word was sent to the men at the other gates to abandon their posts and come to the front.

Just when it appeared hopeless, the Micorites appeared.

17

Victory?

Having defeated the expected defense force of Olympus-Gorfulu, the Italians soldiers began to spread out. Their plan was for a small force to take control of the power plant while the remainder herded the defeated Earthmen to the city square, where they could be more easily controlled. They were unaware of the Micorian population of the domed city, and the sudden appearance of such a huge force took them by surprise.

The defeated Earthmen of Olympus-Gorfulu recognized the newcomers as *bilal* – slaves. There were subtle differences in dress between the slave caste and the free men of Micor, which the Earthmen had learned over their weeks of cohabitation with the natives of Bronson Beta. There were no soldiers among the Micorites, and only the *bilal* had any experience in physical activities, primarily the Games (not all of which had lethal endings for the losers; professionals were recruited from amateur ranks; and, only certain special games had fatal consequecnes for the losers). They were the closest thing Micorian society had to fighting men.

Prodded by their masters, the *bilal* charged the invading Italians. They did so with various hand tools, or implements that could be used as weapons. The Micorites surged forward in wave after wave, seemingly heedless of their lives, and were cut down by Italian bullets in wave after wave. But even the determined invaders, with their modern weaponry, could not kill faster than the ranks of *bilal* were replenished: There were two hundred Italians – less now, after fighting their way into the city – and thousands of *bilal*. Italian positions were overrun. The fighting became even more brutal as it turned to hand to hand combat.

Overrun, three Italian soldiers were forced to retreat, shooting pursuers as they did so. Away from the main fighting, they successfully eluded death at the hands of the *bilal*, losing themselves on a side street that was quiet except for the echoes of battle from the west. But they didn't stop for a respite. They kept moving. Nova Roma – the name given to the Micorian city the Italians had colonized – still had a chance. It all depended upon capturing the power plant. From there, conquerors could demand surrender, and get it.

They found the layout of Olympus-Gorfulu virtually identical to that of Nova Roma, which is what they had expected, what the entire Italian strategy had counted on. That plan called for more than three soldiers to assault the power plant, which might or might not be defended. But the trio of men had no idea if those assigned the mission could carry it out. It seemed unlikely, for the arrival of the natives drastically changed the odds of battle.

Speaking among themselves, the three men deduced the identity of the newcomers. "You know who those strange ones must be," one prompted his companions.

The soldier next to him, who was a rather burly fellow, nodded. "The ones who lived here before. They awoke here."

When settling the newfound city, the Italians encountered the "Early Risers", as Duquesne had dubbed them, among the sleeping Micorites, and killed them. They then destroyed the machines beneath Nova Roma, killing twenty million natives in their slumber chambers.

"We've failed," said the third. "We must flee, or be killed or captured."

"We still have a chance," said one of his brother soldiers.

"We should call a general retreat and re-group in Nova Roma," insisted the third. He abruptly stopped his march. "I'm going to find a radio and do just that." Without waiting for his two comrades, he stalked away in a determined manner.

"Well?" asked the soldier who had started the conversation.

"Let's continue," said the other. "The Earthmen have no machine guns, and the natives have no guns of any type. Surely, there is not an army waiting at the power plant."

"No," agreed the first. "Surely there is not." He suddenly felt better about the task he had chosen. "Let's go."

The two men, who had halted when their comrade had departed, resumed their march toward the power plant of the city.

There was not much fighting, away from the two westernmost gates. The two Italian soldiers had no trouble making their way through the deserted streets of the city. Anyone who was not fighting had stayed inside. Almost everyone.

The two men came upon a middle-aged Micorian male, swathed in his loose cloak-like garb of a dark, neutral hue. One of the Italians raised his machine gun.

"Wait!" the other barked. "He's only an old man."

"So?"

"So, don't waste your ammunition. And the noise may bring others."

"*He* may warn others to our presence," the other soldier objected.

"True," the first speaker agreed. "Use your knife."

Pulling his knife from its sheath, the soldier advanced on the middle-aged fellow, who seemed frozen in fear. Actually, he was sluggish with curiosity at the Italian invaders, this being his first real look at any of them.

He raised a hand as the Italian soldier approached him, knife on display to show his intent. Now, up close, the invader could see the older fellow was not afraid. His worn face held a look of determination. His mouth was set.

A sharp pain suddenly stabbed at the advancing soldier's head. It was a headache worse than he had ever experienced, as if someone was driving a needle into his brain. He had never experienced a migraine before, but he had heard of them, and concluded that what was happening to him must be one.

The Italian faltered. It was hard to think – even hard to see. It hurt just to keep his eyes open. He squeezed them shut in hopes of reducing his pain. This helped, a little, he thought, but he couldn't be sure, the pain was so great.

"What's wrong?" asked him comrade, a few feet behind. He got no answer. He saw his fellow soldier begin to stagger, moving about aimlessly. The knife fell to the metal-like street, clanking as it hit, as he took his heads in his hands. He was monaing now, one contunous sound of misery and suffering. It reminded his comrade of men on the battlefield who lay dying. It was an awful sound, one not easily forgotten.

"Luigi!" called out the other. He got no response as his comrade staggered about blindly. Animal noises were coming from Luigi Sicarelli. They were unreasoning sounds of pain.

The unafflicted soldier moved forward to determine what was wrong. He had seen nothing to cause the strange behavior in his comrade.

As he came forward, the elderly native man shifted his gaze to the newcomer.

Then sharp pain like a hot knife stabbed at the soldier's brain.

Elsewhere in the city, the tide had turned.

Dead bodies littered the streets of Olympus-Gorfulu like autumn leaves that had fallen when it was all over. Fifty Earthmen had been killed, along with a thousand *bilal*. Half of the two hundred Italians were killed in their assault, most at the hands of the Micorian slaves. The majority of the survivors were badly wounded. Only a handful had escaped, retreating to their larks and taking off before the Argonauts could mount any pursuit.

When Jack Taylor pressed Peter Vanderbilt about giving chase, the head of security said, "Let them go. They don't matter. We won."

18

Raid on Nova Roma

Once the battle was over, Tony Drake threw himself into organizing the chaos that had occurred in Olympus-Gorfulu. Triage was the first priority, assessing the wounded and getting them treatment. The little hospital was overwhelmed with patients, and all staff had been called in as soon as the wounded started pouring in. They worked through Light Night and into Dark Day, saving more than half their patients. Micorian medicine, like all of the natives' sciences, was more advanced than Earth medicine, and everyone who still possessed a spark of life when they arrived at the hospital was saved. These numbered in the hundreds, and an adjacent building was commandeered for the overflow.

A tally of the dead was taken. Tony Drake was preparing the list for announcement later that day when Peter Vanderbilt came into the hall of the Central Authority. "The guns have been gathered and placed into the arsenal," he said. "If the Italians return, we'll be well prepared."

"We should have been better prepared," Tony confessed bitterly. "I didn't expect them to breach the dome so easily."

"Maltby and Von Bietz are looking over their lock-picking machine," Peter said, ignoring the opportunity to either condemn or console his leader. The ingenius device had been abandoned in the mad retreat of the survivors.

Tony gazed up at the gray-haired man, catching Peter's blue eyes with his own. "We've been complacent. There's no reason we couldn't have built such a device – or one to counter it."

Peter shrugged. "It's been a hard year. We've faced and overcome one problem after another. You can't blame anyone for not wanting to think about a new problem. And, it's as you said – the dome is fairly unbreachable. We might not have foreseen a lock-picking machine even if we'd concentrated on developing Micorian technology.

"Look at how complacent *they* are. They could easily build such a machine and they didn't. Didn't even *suggest* such a thing. They haven't done much since they awoke a month ago." Peter referred to Bronson Beta months, each of which was forty-one Bronson Beta days, or just over eighty-five Earth days.

A small smile came upon Tony's handsome face. "Thanks."

"For what?"

"For the pep talk."

"Oh, is that what it was?" Peter smiled wanly. "I thought I was stating facts."

This brought a small laugh from Tony Drake, which promptly disappeared when Dave Ransdell entered the chamber, a stern look upon his handsome face, which looked as if it belonged on a statue of the ancient Greeks, so perfect was it, even in turmoil. He strode purposefully toward the two men.

"What is it, Dave?" Tony asked.

"I just heard you're not planning on mounting a counter offensive," the South African gritted.

"That's right," answered Tony. "Their force has been decimated, and now they know they're outnumbered. I doubt they'll be back."

"You're wrong, Tony," Dave announced firmly. It was almost an accusation. "Mussolini will see us as a threat now, not just a rival power. He'll realize that the longer he waits to attack, the worse his odds: Our population will grow exponentially compared to his. He'll *have* to attack again.

"And next time, I'm betting he'll bring weapons built using Micorian technology. The weapons they mounted on the larks are amazing. If they turned them into handheld weapons, they'd be unstoppable. They'd have won the battle despite the *bilal*, if each soldier had carried a machine gun like those weapons."

"What did you have in mind, Dave?" Tony asked, keeping his tone neutral.

"We might be able to negotiate with him, but that would probably only be a delaying tactic on his part. I suggest attacking the Italians now, to show him we're not taking his aggression lying down. We're not weak, we're not cowards. We have to show him that we're too powerful for him, and it's in the best interest of his people to leave us alone."

"How do you propose to do that?" Peter asked, curious about Dave's ideas. "We'll have the same problem the Italians had – getting in through the dome. Are you thinking of taking their lock-picking machine and using it against them?"

The South African explorer shook his head. "No. Our objective is not the same as the Italians'. They wanted to control our city – we just want to show them that they shouldn't mess with us. I have an idea to do this that doesn't call for costly ground fighting."

Dave Ransdell began outlining his plan of attack on Nova Roma.

Several days later, an air raid warning sounded in the domed city occupied by the Italians. The Nova Romans, confirming the alert by human senses, sighted a squadron of colorful larks from Olympus-Gorfulu. They scrambled their own planes in response, intending to shoot down the enemy craft out of the greenish Bronson Beta sky.

They quickly took the metal birds up in expert fashion. Since their occupation of the Micorian city, the Italians had drilled ceaselessly with the advanced planes, until they were as skilled as they had been with Earth ships. The pilot corps, which had flown ground troops to Olympus-Gorfulu, had served as reinforcements in that battle, and so their contingent was largely intact. Two dozen airmen responded to the invading larks, and the first air war of Bronson Beta began.

19

Dance of the Larks

When Baron Manfred von Richthofen, a German pilot of the Great War, had his Fokker Albatross painted crimson in 1917, he became known as the Red Baron. The pilots under his command soon followed suit, and became known as the Flying Circus, due to the bright colors of their planes, as well as their mobile status and use of tents, which was reminiscent of a traveling carnival. The battle of the larks over Nova Roma resembled the Red Baron's flying circus, not only for the flashing colors, but for the sounds and hectic activity that accompanied the buzzing planes.

Diverting his attention from the chaos all around him, Dave Ransdell observed that the Italians had improved the efficiency of Nova

Roma's airfield by removing all the buildings that stood between it and the nearest gate. They had also added a second path so that both northern gates now served as runways. This reduced the time it took to get a plane into the air by minutes, minutes that could mean the difference between victory and defeat.

A rueful grimace came over the South African's handsome face as considered that he should have thought of this himself. He decided that he was going to have to overhaul Olympus-Gorfulu's aerodrome when this was all over.

A sudden jarring sensation brought him back to reality. The tail end of his lark had almost been sheared off by the machine gun-like weapon of an Italian pilot. These fired metal darts propelled by powerful electromagnetism, traveling at a velocity far faster than that of terrestrial bullets. The darts were twisted into a spiral, resembling a finned drill bit or dull-looking Christmas ornament, to make them fly true. A volley of them could disintegrate a plane constructed of even Micorian steel in a matter of seconds.

The invaders had left some of their planes behind when they'd retreated – their pilots having been killed – and Dave, as head of the counter offensive, had been put in charge of the foreign larks. Maltby, a mechanic, and von Bietz and Williamson, electrical engineers, had studied the advanced weapons on the Italian planes and duplicated them. The ships of Olympus-Gorfulu were quickly outfitted with these astonishing guns.

Ransdell pushed his lark – the yellow and black one that he had taken from the very city below him weeks earlier – into a steep dive. He fought the plane as it descended – the damaged tail was giving him trouble, but he kept control of the ship. Not only was he an expert pilot before coming to Bronson Beta, but the explorer was by far the most experienced flyer with Micorian craft. He knew better than anyone what a lark could do.

The Italian pilot followed, but hesitantly, afraid of not being able to pull out of such a steep dive.

Ransdell counted on this fear, and gave his plane everything the motor *could* give, soon outpacing the less experienced pursuer. He came back up into the greenish sky to find himself behind a green, white and red Italian job. He disintegrated it with his E-M (electro-magnetic) gun before the pilot knew what had happened. He couldn't have lived for more than few seconds after being struck by one of Ransdell's well-placed darts, and was in shock, unfeeling of the pain that accompanied the horrendous wound caused by the fast-moving darts: The young Italian had nearly been torn in two.

Leonid Malinkov was not much of a pilot but he believed in the cause. He was one of the Russians who had come to Bronson Beta as part of the Asiatic alliance, which consisted of Soviets, German socialists and like-minded Japanese who opposed the militarism of their government, which had begun gobbling up portions of mainland Asia recently. Unlike many of his comrades, Malinkov was a Menshevik, that faction of Russian

Communism which believed in peaceful progress, not violent revolution as the Bolsheviks preached. He'd been happy to see the end of the war between the Asiatic alliance and the Americans, despite his side having lost. Life in Olympus-Gorfulu was an idyllic existence, not unlike the workers' paradise Karl Marx envisioned. There were no czars, no masters, no overlords, and without the need for wealth, greed was largely absent from Bronson Beta.

As a socialist, Malinkov, who liked to tell people that he had been named after Leon Trotsky, though this claim was somewhat dubious, was a sworn enemy of fascism wherever it existed – even on a new world.

Having passed his probationary period after the peaceful members of the Asiatic alliance were brought into the fold, Malinkov was accepted for pilot training. He was not an armchair patriot, and wished to take an active part in the defense of his home. Born in 1909, he was too young to have participated in the October Revolution. He joined the Red Army when he came of age to protect Russia, but the status quo soon changed with the sighting of the Bronson bodies in 1931.

The ark of the Asiatic alliance had been a people's project – for the people, by the people and of the people. It attracted a group of men and women who each contributed what they could to the project, even if that was just a strong back. Strong backs were needed for such a massive undertaking, the construction of a ship that could safely journey through space to another world.

When the Soviet government learned of it, they intended to appropriate it. They planned for the Soviet elite, including Josef Stalin, to escape the dying Earth in their own ark, but their tests with atomic motors failed. Russia was still a backwards country, technologically, partly because it had been primitive under the last czar, and partly because Stalin mistrusted scientists, and therefore science itself. The Soviet ark was doomed to failure before it was even begun.

The cream of Soviet ideology itself seemed doomed. Few other nations were friendly to Soviet Russia, and none cared to make space for the elite members of the country. News of the other ark, located in northern China where there was no law, was a godsend to men who believed in no god.

The Red Army was sent in. When they realized the true state of things, they abandoned their mission and joined the alliance, providing protection against external threats during the construction phase. There was little of this, consisting mostly of an occasional Chinese bandit and more Red Army troops, sent to investigate what had happened to the earlier force that had seemingly disappeared. A bitter battle ensued, and the invaders had been repelled. This was how Leonid Malinkov had earned his seat on the ark.

He was a mediocre pilot at best, but he fought fiercely against the fascist Italian pilots, using every trick that Dave Ransdell, who was an expert flyer, had taught him, firing the guns made with Micorian technology. The Russian dived and swooped and rolled his lark, unable to elude a superior Italian pilot.

Leonid Malinkov was the first Argonaut to die in the air battle over Nova Roma.

Young Jack Taylor spotted Dave Ransdell's lark: It was the only one painted yellow and black, and thus easy to locate. He had lost sight of it in the fight – his first. The South African had paired as many veterans – these were mostly British – with novices as he was able. Despite the skill of some of the newcomers to flying, aerial combat was an altogether different proposition. Knowing the redhead's importance to Tony Drake, Dave had taken the graduate student under his wing. He was a good pilot and a brave young man, and a battle would season him – if he survived. Dave intended to see that he did. But the two had become separated in the chaos of flitting little planes spewing deadly darts.

When the Italian ships came up, they did so in a strange formation. Few in the Argonaut force recognized it for what it was: the finger-four formation, which had been developed by the Finnish Air Force in 1934 as part of their defense program against potentially hostile neighbors as the situation on Earth grew dire. This divided a squadron of sixteen planes into four groupings of four each. Each of the four groupings consisted of a two-plane lead element and a two-plane second element. The four planes were positioned in such a way as to resemble the fingers of a hand; hence, the formation's name. The flight leader would take lead position, with his partner to his left rear. To the right rear was the element leader, with his own partner to his right rear. Both leaders took offensive roles in combat, the only ones to attack enemy aircraft until the formation breaks up, while their partners played defense, covering the rears of their leaders. This proved quite effective, rapidly decimating the numerically superior Argonaut force.

Two of the Italian larks were now on Jack Taylor's tail. He was helpless – all he could do was run and hope for the best. Soon, his plane was virtually useless, much of it shot away by the EM gun of the lead pursuer. He had somehow escaped being shot himself, and the young man knew that this was more due to luck than any skill he might possess as a pilot.

Jack also knew he didn't have long to live. His lark was going down, and he couldn't stop it. He was losing maneuverability fast. If he hadn't been pursued, he might have a chance at bringing the plane safely down, but he'd be shot out of the sky long before he could do that. He expected death at any moment.

But it never came.

Suddenly, the air was still and the cockpit was quiet once more, the way it had been before he'd engaged the Italians. Jack spun his red-crested head around – and saw Dave Ransdell's yellow and black lark behind him! The South African had shot down both Italian pursuers!

Both Peter Vanderbilt and Jack Taylor were among Olympus-Gorfulu's pilots. They, along with Tony Drake, had been Dave Ransdell's first students, months ago. Then, after weeks of training, they, too, became teachers, passing on what they'd learned at the hands of a master.

Nicky Caswell was one of the few men flying in the air battle over Nova Roma who had been a pilot on Earth. With his experience in the Great War, he had been the natural choice to lead the second squadron of larks – Dave Ransdell naturally led the first. The primary duty of this second squadron was "bomber escort", which meant they were to protect their wards: Three large transport planes followed behind the two waves of fighters.

After the dog fighting had begun and was well under way, the three giants arrived.

The Italians could not know, could not even guess, what lay within the three large transport planes. But they knew it was something extraordinary, something unusual – something *special*. They had used the bigger planes to transport ground troops, and assumed the same of the Argonauts – with their superior numbers, a land invasion made sense. Nova Roma would be easily overwhelmed. For all the Italians knew, the three ships were but the first of many. Thus, air traffic control re-directed the pilots from engaging the enemy larks to shooting down the three transports.

The flyers of Olympus-Gorfulu saw their opponents break off their devastating attack and flee – at least, that's what it looked like to novice pilots. It struck them as odd – the Argonaut air force was on the ropes. It wouldn't take long for the Italians to finish them off. It didn't make sense that they were running – flying – away.

But experienced pilots like Dave Ransdell knew better. His cool blue eyes went to the three big planes and their lark escorts, and realized why the Italians' strategy had suddenly changed. It was vital to his plan that the trio of transports get through and do their job. Into his radio, he barked, "This is it, boys! We've got to stop them from shooting down the transports!"

20

Peace Comes to Bronson Beta

When the Italians saw the beam of bright hot light shoot out of the first transport, they knew what it was, recognized its destructive brilliance. It was like looking into the Sun. This was not far from the truth, for the light issued forth from a cannon fashioned from one of the atomic motors of an ark.

There was no bomb in existence that could breach the transparent metal of the domes of the Micorian cities. They had been designed and constructed to survive the fast-moving particulate matter of open space. They served as the second defense ring of Bronson Beta, the first being the planet's atmosphere.

The three large ships carried the only weapon known to be able to pierce the transparent barrier: the atomic motors that had propelled the arks to Bronson Beta. They produced a plasma with a heat in excess of nine thousand degrees Fahrenheit, enough to melt any metal on Earth – even, after a time, Ransdellium, which had been used to line the engines' tubes. One of the four motors of the smaller ark, which had been under the command of Cole Hendron himself, had been converted into a furnace for the Colony; its tube had been used by Tony Drake and Eliot James in an exploratory pod, and damaged. Without the tube, the exiles could never turn the engine into a weapon, and they needed it as a source of electricity. It also provided heat for their enclosure via the ark's electric heaters.

While the engines of the second, larger ark commanded by Dave Ransdell were intact, the four tubes of it were damaged in flight, causing the ship to crash land, and were then further damaged *in* the crash. They were all but useless (though the Ransdellium had been recycled and re-purposed). That left three tubes from the smaller of the two arks, *Noah's Ark*. Each of these, with a motor, was fitted into one of the large planes, which, despite the size of the craft, was a tight squeeze and took a bit of doing. The engineers had also had to add an extra layer of insulation to protect the planes from the intense heat of the plasma beam. This was where the recycled Ransdellium came in.

Two of the transport planes opened their large cargo doors and, aiming their cannons at the dome, began firing, while the third flew on. A pair of larks escorted it through Nova Roman air space as the two forces joined in battle around the big transports.

Seeing that the Italian pilots had abandoned defense in order to wage an all-out assault on the three transports, the Argonaut flyers pursued. They did so somewhat recklessly, as they had been told of the importance of the three cannon-bearing craft. Fortunately, they had no pursuers to capitalize on their carelessness.

The Italian larks were slaughtered. But the pilots were good enough that a few got through the defense of the Argonaut larks under the command of Nicky Caswell and destroyed one of the pair of transports over their city. It crashed into the trees some distance away, killing all aboard. Everything in the sky was now focused on the remaining transport, either protecting it or bringing it down.

Larks swarmed about the sole ship as its atomic plasma cannon cut a swath through the dome below. Now, the Italians knew, their new city would be exposed to the bitter cold of the Bronson Beta winter, dooming them. Still, the fight was not lost: If they could stop the damage before it grew too severe, it could be repaired before winter came. They already possessed some knowledge of how to manipulate Micorian steel.

But the fight to bring down the cannon was a bitter one. There were heavy losses on both sides. Dave Ransdell became the first ace on Bronson Beta that day, but he wasn't the only one. If the Italians had not abandoned their attack to shoot down the transports, they would have won the air battle, due to their superior flying skills. Until that point, they had downed more larks than had the Argonauts.

Suddenly, the South African's voice thundered over the radios of the larks: "Action avalanche! Repeat: action avalanche!" This was directed at the remaining planes under his command.

One by one, the survivors dived down at the dome. But rather than attacking it, they swooped into the large hole made by the two atomic cannons and began firing at the Italian planes being readied for take off. These were in a row like an assembly line, for in truth that was what it was.

The fighter larks of Olympus-Gorfulu had never stood a chance against the Italians, who possessed more pilots who were also better pilots. Dave Ransdell's plan all along had been to cripple Nova Roma's air force, not destroy the city's protective dome.

The green, white and red planes were sitting ducks on the ground. The South African's pilots ruined the entire line of the larks in three passes at them, as pilots and ground crew fled for cover. The metal darts destroyed everything they hit.

When this was done, the five planes – out of an original twenty-four – proceeded to destroy the entire airfield, one building at a time, using their EM guns with their metal-penetrating darts.

By the time Dave Ransdell and the others returned to the greenish sky over Nova Roma, the air battle was over. The Italians had been soundly defeated and the single transport was already headed back toward Olympus-Gorfulu.

"Your plan worked great!" Jack Taylor enthused as he wrestled to keep his lark in the sky

– he had missed the end of the battle and the run on the Nova Roman aerodrome.

"I second that," came Nicky Caswell's voice over the radio. "Brilliant strategy."

"That should take care of them for quite a while," added Peter Vanderbilt.

The destruction of the airfield effectively ended the ability of the Nova Romans to wage war. Without transports to ferry soldiers to Olympus-Gorfulu, a ground war was virtually impossible. The Italians hadn't mapped the land to the east, and without a road, they would have trouble locating their target. If they bothered to attempt to march almost seven thousand miles with an army of less than two hundred.

They could not replace their lost planes with those from one of the other surviving domed cities of the west: These had already been retrieved by the Argonauts, in the first phase of Dave Ransdell's plan, while Olympus-Gorfulu's experts duplicated the Italians' EM guns.

The threat of Nova Roma was ended for the foreseeable future.

The third transport, which had broken off from the assault on Nova Roma and continued its flight, arrived at its destination before the air battle had ended. Twenty minutes after the plane had left the domed city's air space, the ark of the Italians came into view. The men inside opened the large bay door, and aimed the atomic cannon at the massive ship below. The bright beam shot out, and the metal craft began to melt under the intense heat.

This was the final phase of Dave Ransdell's plan: Destroy the atomic motors of the Italian ark so that the same attack could not be used against Olympus-Gorfulu in the future.

21

Quarantine

The burden of leadership was sometimes an awful weight. At the moment, Tony Drake was only too aware that his duty to attend a peace conference with Benito Mussolini prevented him from being present at the birth of his child: Eve Hendron was due any day now, a few days after the Battle of Nova Roma, as it was being called in Olympus-Gorfulu. The baby was late, as first children sometimes are, and there was no predicting when it would arrive, not even with the advanced technology of the Micorites.

The transport plane arrived early in the morning, soon after dawn, and was expected to be on its way before Dark Day began some twenty-five hours later. The leader of the Argonauts did not trust Il Duce, and did not plan to partake of his hospitality overnight. In fact, he planned to spend as little time as possible in Nova Roma, which had nothing to do with his wife's condition. This was the rational part of his decision. The emotional part beckoned him home for the birth of his daughter, and this was the more pressing of the two to Tony.

Tony did not go blindly into the lair of wolves: Philbin, the linguist, had questioned the Italian prisoners of war. Some were more helpful than others, proud of Il Duce and the Italians' accomplishments since arriving on Bronson Beta.

Tony had not expected to learn much – there didn't seem much to learn – and he was not surprised. He prepared for the worst: A small contingent of reserve volunteers who had proven themselves in battle, now led by Kyto, formerly Tony Drake's manservant, came with him in the transport plane. They were armed with personal EM guns – though considerably smaller than the variety mounted on the larks, they were still quite large, about the size of a Browning Automatic Rifle.

The rifles made an impression on the Nova Romans, who had not thought such a reduction in size possible. But, they did not have Micorian engineers working with them, as the Earthmen of Olympus-Gorfulu had. The natives of Bronson Beta were wizards with technology.

Tony Drake and his men were met at one of the eastern gates by an honor guard. They wore uniforms, similar to that of the Italian Army, but woven on Bronson Beta with Bronson Beta fibers.

The colorful regalia of the uniform were quite eye-catching. Mussolini was something of a showman, no less so on the new Earth than the old.

One soldier stepped forward and said, in English, "Greetings from Il Duce. If you follow us, we will take you to him for the signing of an historic treaty of peace between our two great nations." This was recited in such a manner that suggested it had been memorized, although the command of English seemed genuine enough. "My name is Teddy. Is there anything you require, Mister Tony Drake, sir?"

"We're fine, thank you," answered Tony. He recognized the name from Dave Ransdell's account, and gestured for Teddy to lead the way.

Teddy Tedeschi spun sharply on his heel and began to lead the procession through the streets of Nova Roma. The contingent from Olympus-Gorfulu was escorted along the wide avenue to a luxurious tower that could be nothing less than Mussolini's personal palace. The soldiers moved with the military precision one expected from a fascist army.

The Argonauts were glad for the escort. It meant that an ambush was unlikely. Mussolini did not have so many men left he could afford to waste them. There were no more than two hundred, according to Dave Ransdell's estimates, half of which were actually women.

Overhead, repair operations to the dome were already underway, conducted by a pair of machines that worked cooperatively. Bright, unfiltered sunlight leaked in through the hole in the dome.

While Teddy opened the double doors of the tower, leading the way into the lobby, the honor guard remained outside, stationed in formation along the sidewalk.

Tony did not release his own men. There was no telling what lay within the tower – there could be a small army waiting for him. He didn't think so, but it never paid to be careless. Leaving half of his men at the elevator, the other half accompanied him up to the waiting Il Duce.

When the elevator door opened – the cage had gone all the way to the top, rising quite rapidly, as did all Micorian elevators – Tony Drake found that Mussolini was indeed not alone. But his companions were not soldiers. They were advisors, or ministers, dressed in civilian clothing. They had the manner of "yes men" as they fussed over Il Duce as though he were a child. When he saw Tony, he impatiently waved them away.

As he entered it behind Teddy, Tony Drake took in the room: It was an anteroom that served as Il Duce's office, with a large desk beside a large window that overlooked the city. If Tony had not gotten his directions mixed up, Mussolini could watch the ruined airfield from this location. The chamber was decorated quite splendidly, in a hybrid of Italian and Micorian style, the latter of which often utilized red and gold in the east. Here it was aquamarine and cream.

"Welcome, Tony Drake," Mussolini smiled. There was a falseness to it that the Italian leader could not hide. "I hope you found your escort worthy of your position."

"It was quite nice," the former stockbroker returned. "I'm very impressed by what you've achieved here."

"Thank you," Mussolini responded sincerely. "Please." He gestured with a beefy hand to chairs separated by a small table that appeared to have been brought in for this special occasion, for it did not fit the decor of the room. Tony took a seat.

The details of the treaty had been worked out by intermediaries over the past few days, though Tony, and doubtless Mussolini, were intimately involved in the negotiations. In exchange for Nova Roma building no air force, Olympus-Gorfulu would cease all hostilities and return its Italian prisoners. There wasn't much more to it than that. There was no trade – each society had everything it needed, and there was no need to speak of a division of land or boundaries with seven thousand miles separating them. In turn, each leader signed two copies of the treaty, without speaking, and each took one.

Standing, Tony Drake extended his hand. "I hope our two cities can be friends."

Il Duce took the hand and shook it. He had a strong grip, but did not exert much pressure on Tony's hand. "I underestimated you. I never make the same mistake twice."

"I hope that means you have no more plans for conquest," Tony said neutrally. "Bronson Beta is large enough for both of our populaces."

"Of course," Mussolini smiled again, that same false smile that Tony had seen earlier. "What else could I mean?"

184

Tony Drake remained diplomatically silent on that topic. He had gotten what he'd come for and was anxious to return home. "I'll see to the return of your men as soon I get back to Olympus-Gorfulu."

"Very well."

As soon as the transport plane was in the air, Tony Drake got on its radio and contacted air traffic control in Olympus-Gorfulu. Jack Taylor was standing by there, possessing the latest update about Eve Hendron. The leader of mankind was informed that his wife had gone to the hospital to have their baby.

Tony urged the pilot to push the advanced motor of the craft. Its speed edged up toward four hundred miles per hour. No one had ever found its upper limit. Tony insisted that they try.

As soon as the plane landed some nine Bronson Beta hours later, Tony Drake bounded from it and climbed into the small car that young Jack had waiting for him. The redhead gunned the motor and the automobile – a blocky, bronze-colored thing – zipped through the streets of Olympus-Gorfulu toward the hospital. This belonged to Jack, who claimed it was the fastest thing on Bronson Beta. He seemed determined to prove this to Tony as he drove. Frequent updates during the flight had assured Tony that he was not too late. Eve was in labor now, but had not yet given birth.

Charles Dodson met Tony at the door to the hospital. With an unabashed grin on his face, he exclaimed, "Your daughter wants to see you."

Tony Drake was too happy at the news to recriminate himself for missing the birth. "Is she all right?"

It was not clear to which "she" he was referring, his wife or his daughter, but Dodson answered, "They're both just fine, Tony. Come on." The one-armed physician turned and led the way inside.

The tiny figure clutched against Eve Hendron's breast was barely recognizable as a human being – but it was – Tony's daughter.

Seeing her husband in the doorway, Eve flashed a beaming smile. She looked exhausted, her copper hair disheveled, her face flushed. Tony rushed to his wife's side. "I'm sorry I missed it."

"It's all right, honey," Eve assured him. "You'd just have been pacing nervously in the waiting room, anyway. What you did today in Nova Roma was important ... crucially important. There's nothing to be sorry about.

"I ...."

"Yes, dear?" Tony asked expectantly.

"I think I've settled on a name."

Tony waited patiently to hear. He had accepted "Nicole", and wondered what Eve meant.

"How do you like Virginia?"

"I like it fine," the former stockbroker answered, surprised by the name. Eve had never mentioned it before. "I like it. What happened to Nicole?"

"It occurred to me that if our next child is a boy, we'll want to use Cole for him. Cole and Nicole, no thank you."

"I like Virginia. How did you come up with it?"

"The first child born in the New World was named Virginia Dare," Eve Hendron explained. "We can honor our heritage by naming our daughter, the first human born on Bronson Beta, after her. Virginia Dare Drake."

"I like it," Tony repeated, a little more forcefully, which showed his genuine sincerity. "Virginia Dare Drake."

Jack Taylor found Tony Drake in the hospital just as the sun was setting and Dark Day was beginning. On Earth, young Jack had been Tony's protégé. On Bronson Beta, he had become Tony's aide-de-camp. He sometimes acted as a buffer between his boss and citizens at large, who often thought their problem the most important in the city. This occasionally put him in the position of being the bearer of bad news.

Jack's face was flushed when he came into the room where Tony and Eve were; baby Virginia was asleep in the nursery now. Tony, sleeping awkwardly in a chair, awoke at Jack's entrance. The ex-college man was not the excitable sort, and if he was excited, Tony knew that it was something big. He slipped noiselessly from the chair and joined Jack in the hall outside.

"What is it?" Tony enquired.

"The Micorites want to talk to you." The young redhead's voice was tight.

"Now? What is it?"

"They say they've found the cause of the Micorian disease that's sweeping the city," Jack explained.

"What do they want me for? Why don't they tell Dr. Dodson? He's working on that case with Anlas Nirol."

"I don't know. But they want to talk to you."

"Okay, let's go," said Tony. "Just let me tell someone I'm leaving so Eve won't be worried when she wakes up."

When this task had been accomplished, the two men left the hospital and returned to Tony's office in the Hall of the Central Authority, where the Micorian doctor Anlas Nirol and another native – a man – a waited in the anteroom. He was older, possessed a regal bearing, and Tony guessed that he was some sort of Micorian leader.

Tony waved a hand upon entering. "Please come in."

Upon everyone seating themselves, Tony Drake said, "Jack says that you've found the cause of the fits of madness that's been plaguing your people."

Anlas Nirol nodded. "That is correct. It comes from you humans."

Tony didn't say anything. The current theory was that some sort of illness was being spread by sexual contact. He waited for more information, wondering why they were telling him – perhaps they wanted some sort of human curfew or something.

"This is Fenic Olo," said Anlas Nirol. "He is the Micorian equivalent of an Earth psychiatrist."

Fenic Olo, who appeared to be middle-aged with an almost lavendar graying to his hair, leaned forward in his chair. "The cause of the madness is not physical, Tony Drake – it is psychic. The human mind is wild and chaotic – untrained. Part of this is due to a slightly different brain structure than we Micorites possess. Prolonged proximity with humans is causing the madness among my people."

"Our presence ... is driving you mad?" Tony asked slowly, unable to believe what he had heard.

"Essentially, yes," answered Fenic Olo. "It is not the sexual contact that had been theorized, but the intense emotions accompanying the act.

"But not only that. Micorites who worked or lived near humans for long periods were also victims of the madness."

Tony Drake reeled at the information. It was unbelievable – but he believed it. "What must be done to stop it?"

"Humans must withdraw from Olympus-Gorfulu."

Over the next few days, this was done. All the Earthmen who lived in Olympus-Gorfulu and the other Micorian cities withdrew. Tony Drake did not have to tell the native representatives that humans could not survive the winter of Bronson Beta without shelter, and he found that a plan had already been devised by the council of Micorians: Hendron-Khorlu, where the Earth farm had been established, would be given to the humans for their own city. Contact between the two races would thereafter be limited, and carefully controlled.

The move was made peacefully, with heavy hearts. The Micorites bore the Earthmen no ill will, for it was not their fault, and the humans were sad to lose their new neighbors.

Dave Ransdell did not make the move to Hendron-Khorlu with his fellow Argonauts. He was off in his repaired yellowjacket lark on another adventure when the Earthmen re-located to their original home on Bronson Beta.

BRONSON BETA
known area

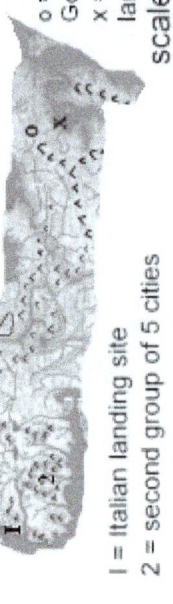

I = Italian landing site
2 = second group of 5 cities

o = Olympus-
Gorfulu
x = American
landing site
scale = [2000 mi]

Chronology of the "Worlds Collide" Trilogy

Although the Foreword of *After Worlds Collide* begins, "Early in the middle third of the twentieth century a brilliant astronomer named Sven Bronson observed through a telescope in South Africa that two bodies were moving through space toward the solar system", this is almost certainly not accurate. This would put the sighting of the Bronson bodies no earlier than 1934.

A number of comments in *When Worlds Collide* suggest that the sighting occurs a bit earlier. For example, as a result of the discovery, "Germany went fascist" (Chapter 9). In reality, this occurred in 1933, meaning that Bronson Alpha and Bronson Beta were sighted in 1931 (this occurred within the year after the announcement, which was a year after the two planets were sighted (CH 9)), meaning that "Germany went fascist" two calendar years after the discovery of the coming planets. Unless you want to posit that on this Earth Germany did not turn to fascism in 1933 as it actually did. I don't.

But that's not the only point.

Three years later, the first pass of the two planets occurs in late July (CH 13). The night of the twenty-eighth "should have been a full moon"

– but the Moon has been obliterated by the encounter with the Bronson planets. The only full moon in the 1930s that occurred near the 28th is in 1934 – it would have been the third night of a full moon; no one in Hendron's camp was outside on the 26th, the actual night of the full moon.

Since 1934 here matches the 1931 from above, 1931 must be the true year that Sven Bronson made his discovery. Or is it?

There is one date that seems to conclusively identify the year that the Bronson Bodies arrive: Christmas. In the year before Earth is destroyed, Eliot James records that they ate Christmas dinner "last Thursday" (CH 21). We would then expect that Christmas fell on a Thursday that year – or perhaps a Friday. But Christmas doesn't fall on a Thursday in any year in the 1930s (or 1940, to be safe). Christmas fell on Friday in 1931 and 1936; therefore, 1936 must be correct. However, the full moon in July in 1936 came on July 4 – nowhere near July 28!

1934 fits better for a number of reasons described above.

Oddly, Eliot James doesn't record the Christmas dinner on the day that it occurs (or if he does, it's not described in the novel). It's possible, that, in his haste, James wrote "Thursday" when he meant "Tuesday", the day Christmas fell on in 1934. I find this to be the most satisfactory explanation.

Now that we have pinpointed the year the Bronson planets arrived, we can begin to apply hard dates to events in the two novels.

When Worlds Collide begins "eleven months" (CH 3) after the discovery. The League of the Last Days was formed by Cole Hendron "six months" earlier (CH 4), during "winter" (CH 2). A "year" after the announcement of the planets, "the end of next summer", when the first passage of the Bronson planets will occur, is "more than a year away" (CH 8), so the story opens a little over two years before the first passing.

After the announcement, Tony Drake is then gone for at least three weeks, recruiting personnel for the League, returning to New York in "July" (CH 9). Tony is sent on another recruiting mission, returning in "late July" (CH 12). There is no reason to think that this assignment was much longer or much shorter than the first, putting his earlier return in early July, and the announcement and the beginning of the novel in mid June. This then places the formation of the League of the Last Days in December, and Bronson's discovery in July – July of 1931.

1931

July	Sven Bronson sights the two Bronson bodies in the southern sky near Achernar. (WWC CH 3)
December	Cole Hendron forms the League of the Last Days with about sixty scientists from around the globe. (WWC CH 2, 4)

1932

mid June   Tony Drake is recruited into the League. (WWC CH 2)

1933

June   The League of the Last Days makes an announcement predicting that the Bronson planets, which can now be seen from the northern hemisphere, will destroy the Earth. Cities are observed on Bronson Beta. (WWC CH 8)

1934

July 25-27   The first pass of the two Bronson planets, as they make their closest approach to Earth, kills half the population. Tidal waves destroy coastal cities on the first day, followed by forty-eight hours of earthquakes, lightning and rainstorms. (WWC CH 13)

The new capital of the United States is now Hutchinson, KS. (WWC CH 16) People and materiel have been diverted to the Mississippi Basin northwest of Kansas since the government

	recognized the threat of the Bronson planets (sometime in the past year). The population of the camp is 14 million at this time.
mid Sept.	Dave Ransdell, one of a trio of surveyors of the new North America, discovers a new metal, brought up from under the Earth's crust, near St. Paul shortly before their return to "Hendronville", in Michigan. (WWC CH 16)
October	Hendronville is attacked. (WWC CH 17-19)
very early Dec.	Hendron announces the idea to construct a second ark. (WWC CH 20)

1935

March 26	The arks are launched. (WWC CH 25)
March 27	The Earth is destroyed when Bronson Alpha strikes it. (WWC CH 26)
March 28	The small ark lands on Bronson Beta in the evening; it is late afternoon on the planet. (WWC CH 26-27) Note: This is four days

before the vernal equinox, the first day of spring. This is therefore four days before the end of the first *calendar* year after arriving on Bronson Beta.

March 30   A number of men sneak out to test Bronson Beta's environment before the official expedition planned for the next morning (March 31). They discover a road. (WWC CH 27)

After Earth year 2

Unum.18-19   The Sleeping Sickness strikes, affecting 26 and killing 3. (AWC CH 3)

Unum. ca. 23   A plane flies over the camp of the first ark. (AWC CH 3)

Duo. 13-15   Tony Drake and Eliot James take a makeshift ship using one of the atomic tubes as an engine and explore the domed city Wend to the west. Looping south, they find the second American ark and make contact. They return to their own camp to find everyone unconscious. It is under attack by the "Midianites", members of an Asiatic alliance consisting of communist Russians, socialist

	Germans and anti-imperialistic Japanese. The invaders are driven off by cannons made from the remaining three atomic motors. Members of both American camps begin the move to the nearest domed city, this one to the south. (AWC CH 5-11)
Duober 16	The migration to the nearest domed city, which is named Hendron, after the leader who died on the journey, is completed. The Central Authority is set up. (AWC CH 13)
Quatt. ca. 5	The Midianites cut off power to Hendron-Khorlu. (AWC CH 17)
Quat. 12-14	A small group of young men invade Midian, while Marian Jackson tricks her way inside, where she kills Seidel, the leader of the Asiatic alliance. This starts a revolt among British prisoners, who take over the city. Eve reveals that she is pregnant. Quattuorber 14 is the winter solstice (and because the calendar is not irregular, always will be). (AWC CH 19-20)

Quin. ca. 30	Dave Ransdell leaves Olympus-Gorfulu to explore the west. (BWC CH 3)
Quin. 41	Preparations for Re-Birth Day begin as Dave Ransdell continues his exploration of the western half of the continent. (BWC CH 1-9)

A.E. 3

Unumber 1	The Re-Birth Day celebration is underway when Dave Ransdell arrives to warn the residents of Olympus-Gorfulu about the Italians. The Micorites under the city begin to awaken. (BWC CH 9)
Unumber ca. 7	Micorite doctor Anlas Nirol volunteers to help the Earthmen cure the Sleeping Sickness. (BWC CH 12)
Unum. ca. 35	The Game is played. After a sumptuous celebration, the losers are ritually executed. (BWC CH 13)
Unum. ca. 36 - Duo. ca. 1	Notor Piyel goes berserk the next day. (BWC CH 13) Over the next several days, more Micorites go berserk, and it becomes suspected that sexual contact with humans might be the cause. (BWC CH 14)

Duo. ca. 2   The Italians attack Olympus-Gorfulu. (BWC CH 14-17)

Duo. ca. 6   The Argonauts attack Nova Roma. (BWC CH 18-20)

Duo. ca. 9   The peace treaty is signed between Olympus-Gorfulu and Nova Roma. Eve Hendron gives birth to her and Tony's baby. The Micorites reveal that the mental illness among their people is caused by close contact with humans, and insist the Earthmen retreat to Hendron-Khorlu, which the natives will abandon. (BWC CH 21)

Duo. ca. 10-12 The humans withdraw from the Micorian cities and take up residence in Hendron-Khorlu. (BWC CH 21)

Jeff Deischer is best known for his chronologically-minded essays, particularly the book-length *The Man of Bronze: a Definitive Chronology*, about the pulp DOC SAVAGE series. It is *a* definitive chronology, rather than *the* definitive chronology, he explains, because each chronologist of the DOC SAVAGE series has his own rules for constructing his own chronology. Jeff believes his own chronology to be the definitive one – using his rules, which were set down by Philip Jose Farmer in his book, *Doc Savage: His Apocalyptic Life*.

Jeff was born in 1961, a few years too late, in his opinion. He missed out on the Beatles, the beginning of the Marvel Age of comic books and the early years of the Bantam reprints of the DOC SAVAGE series, the latter two of which he began reading when he was about ten years old (on the other hand, he was too young to go to Viet Nam ….).

Jeff had become enamored of Heroes – with a capital "H", for these were not *ordinary* men – at a very young age. He grew up watching DANIEL BOONE (to whom he is distantly related, by marriage), TARZAN, BATMAN, THE LONE RANGER and ZORRO on television. There is a large "Z" carved into his mother's sewing machine that can attest to this fact (as you might imagine, it did not impress her the way it always did the peasants and soldiers on ZORRO).

This genre of fiction made a lasting impression on his creative view, and everything he writes has Good Guys and Bad Guys – in capital letters. As an adult writer, he tries to make his characters *human*, as well.

Jeff began writing as a young teenager, and, predictably, all of it was bad. He started to write seriously while in college, but spent the next decade creating characters and universes and planning stories without seeing much of it to fruition. This wasted time is his biggest regret in life.

In the early 1990s, Jeff began a correspondence with noted pulp historian and novelist Will Murray, while he was writing both the DOC SAVAGE and THE DESTROYER series (THE DESTROYER #102 is actually dedicated to Jeff). Jeff currently consults on Will Murray's DOC SAVAGE books (as evidenced by the acknowledgements pages in the novels of "The Wild Adventures of ..." series), a privilege that he enjoys. Will Murray's sage advice helped turn Jeff into a true author.

Producing few books over the next few years, Jeff's writing finally attained professional grade, and, after being laid off from the auto industry in 2007, he was able to devote more time to writing. From 2008, he produced an average of three books a year, most of it fiction, and most of that pulp. Reading so much of the writing of Lester Dent, the first, most prolific and best of those using the DOC SAVAGE house name "Kenneth Robeson", Jeff's own natural style is similar to Dent's. He "turns this up" when writing pulp, and "turns this down" when writing non-pulp fiction.

Jeff primarily writes fiction, and, combining his twin loves of superheroes and pulp, began THE

GOLDEN AGE series in 2012. This resurrected, revamped and revitalized the largely forgotten characters of Ned Pines' Standard, Better and Nedor publishing companies. These characters, drawn from superhero, pulp and mystic milieus, fill the "Auric Universe", as Jeff calls it. In 2015, he started documenting his own Argentverse, filled with characters of his own creation. It is a nostalgic look back on the comic books he read as a young teenager.

Jeff's webpage is jeffdeischer.blogspot.com, where he posts the first chapters of his novels, so that potential readers can peruse his work without having to spend several dollars on a trade paperback to find out if they like it or not.

The Westerntainment Library

Non-Fiction
Over the Rainbow: a User's Guide to My *Dangyang* by Jeff Deischer
The Marvel Timeline Project, Part 1 by Jeff Deischer and Murray Ward
The Way They Were: the Histories of Some of Adventure Fiction's Most Famous Heroes and Villains by Jeff Deischer
The Adventures of the Man of Bronze: a Definitive Chronology (3rd ed.) by Jeff Deischer

Superhero Fiction
The Overman Paradigm by Kim Williamson
The Golden Age, Volume II: Mystico by Jeff Deischer
The Golden Age, Volume III: Dark of the Moon by Jeff Deischer
The Golden Age, Volume IV by Jeff Deischer
The Golden Age, Volume X: Future Tense by Jeff Deischer
The Golden Age, Volume XI: Bad Moon Rising by Jeff Deischer
The Steel Ring by R. A. Jones
The Twilight War by R. A. Jones
Argent by Jeff Deischer
Night of the Owl (Argent) by Jeff Deischer
The Superlatives (Argent) by Jeff Deischer
Strange Days (Argent) by Jeff Deischer
Modern Times (Argent) by Jeff Deischer
Mystery Men (Argent) by Jeff Deischer

Science Fiction
Brave New World: Divided We Planetfall by Lawrence V. Bridgeport

The Brotherhood of Sabours Book One: The Shadow of the Sund by Wes T. Salem
The Brotherhood of Sabours Book Two: The Reavers of Kargh by Wes T. Salem
The Brotherhood of Sabours Book Three: The Red Brotherhood by Wes T. Salem
The Heart of the Universe by Wes T. Salem

Pulp Fiction
Spook Trail by Jeff Deischer
The Winter Wizard by Jeff Deischer
The Little Book of Short Stories: 9 Weird Tales by Jeff Deischer
Red, as in Ruin (Nemesis Company #1) by Jeff Deischer

Other Fiction
Skull & Bones (Agent Keats #1) by John Francis
Chinese Puzzle (Agent Keats #2) by John Francis
High Hopes (Agent Keats #3) by John Francis

www.ingramcontent.com/pod-product-compliance
Lightning Source LLC
LaVergne TN
LVHW011450230325
806616LV00042B/1482